RUIN

HAWKS MC
NEXT GENERATION

USA TODAY BESTSELLING AUTHOR
LILA ROSE

First Edition 2021
ISBN: 978-0-6487998-6-3

PROLOGUE

RUIN

"Enter," Talon called. I opened the door and stepped through with Coyote, my closest brother in the club, at my back. Already in the office were Griz, Blue, Vicious, Killer, Stoke, and Cowboy. Cowboy was a younger member, just twenty-one—a good guy who helped Coyote out at his Harley store.

"You should be restin'," Talon told Coyote. The guy had not long been in a car wreck with his bakery girl after some thugs tried to take them out. It was lucky I'd arrived when I had, with the brothers not far behind. Coyote stared the prez—his dad—down, earning a snort from Talon. "Yeah, I'd be the fuckin' same." We all knew what he meant. He'd still keep going to deal with the fuckers we'd caught.

"Heard from their leader?" Coyote asked.

Talon answered, "We're expectin' a call any second, since Killer used one of the guys' phones and sent a video of one of the captives gettin' worked over."

"They tell you anythin'?" I asked.

Griz snorted. "Sang like cockatoos."

"You mean canaries," Cowboy said.

Griz glared. "What?"

"The sayin' is sang like canaries." When Griz just stared Cowboy down, he added, "But it doesn't matter what kind of bird it is."

Blue snickered while my dad, Stoke, flat-out laughed.

"What did they say?" Coyote asked, wincing when he moved the wrong way.

"Sit before you fall down, Coyote." Talon eyed his son, nodding to the chair in front of his desk.

"Apparently the main guy, whose name's Cub, was goin' after Channa on his own. He roped those guys into helpin' because he wanted payback on her since she made him look like a little pussy," Dad explained.

"Did they say what they think we stole off them?" I asked, since I got the feeling they only attacked after the bakery girl made a fool of them in the first scuffle outside her place.

"All he said was that we'd have to take it up with their leader. But if that fucker doesn't tell us what it is, we'll do some more work on the guys we have. I want this finished by the time night falls." Talon rapped his knuckles on the worn oak desk.

"Agreed," Coyote stated coldly, alongside a few of the other brothers.

The phone rang, pausing the conversation. We shared a look before Talon put it on speaker. "Speak," he ordered.

"This is Wolf. I'm the leader of the Takahashi family and see you have some of my men."

"I'm not sure what you're talkin' about." Talon's voice was guarded. In case the phone call was compromised, he couldn't say too much. "But how about we meet and sort a few things out?"

There was silence for a few beats. "I'm out the front of the compound." The call ended, and shock rocked through us all.

Blue's eyebrows shot high. "He's got some damn big balls."

"He does. Let's go see what he has to say." Talon stood, and we followed him outside. Other members tried to join, but Talon told them to stay back. When we neared the locked gate, a lone man stood on the other side.

This Wolf guy, who had an Asian background, didn't look like he belonged to a thug gang. A mobster one, yeah, with his crisp white suit, black shirt, and long jacket. His long dark hair was neatly tied at the back of his neck. His eyes told a whole other story. Confidence mixed with something a little crazy bled through their depths.

"Talon, I presume?" He even didn't sound like a damn gang member. Each word was clear and correct.

"Yeah, and you're Wolf." Talon stopped just on the other side of the gate and crossed his arms over his chest. "You've come alone."

He nodded. "In good faith."

Blue snorted. "Good faith? After one of yours caused not one, but fuckin' two crashes *and* near-deaths of some of ours?"

Wolf's jaw clenched. "Cub acted alone. He's... let's say... unruly. I never wanted anyone hurt. I only ordered him to ask questions, but he has something against your club that isn't a part of my gang. I reside in Melbourne and have a few members who travel from here to the city. Cub was one of them. It was lucky I was in town checking on them when the situation happened."

"You sayin' he went out on his own for all this shit?" Talon asked.

"Yes."

Talon's silence told us he wasn't sure whether to believe this guy. Still, Talon put his hands on his waist. "He has to pay for what he's done. Two brothers are injured, and so is a woman who's under the club's protection. He was going to *kill* them all if he had his damn way."

"I wouldn't think he'd kill—"

"He had a gun to a brother's head. A gun to the woman's, and everyone who was there could see the intent in his fuckin' eyes. He was gonna kill them. If you don't believe that, I can give you the reports on the damn injuries. *No one* gets away with hurtin' anyone in Hawks."

Wolf's nostrils flared, and the hands at his sides fisted. "Fucking fool," he snarled to the ground. He looked up and met Talon's hard gaze. "He's yours."

"What?" Talon's brows shot up in surprise. I wouldn't have seen it if I wasn't standing beside him.

"Do with him what you will. He acted alone, thinking he could climb the ladder by doing something foolish without consequences. He was wrong. Punish him however you choose. I don't want problems with the Hawks MC, just an answer."

Talon ignored the last part and asked, "The others that were with him?"

"Three, I believe?"

Talon nodded.

"They were stupid to follow Cub in the first place. Put fear in them, and then if they haven't done anything to anyone in your club, release them."

"You want us to teach them a lesson?" Griz asked.

Who the fuck was this guy?

"If you believe they need it, yes."

"Who the fuck are you?" Talon barked. "And what do you think we stole off you?"

He smiled. It was only slight but still there. "As I said, I am Wolf. I control a large part of Melbourne, the women, drugs, and weaponry. I have seen what the Hawks MC can do. I want you to know we don't have an issue with one another unless you get involved in my business."

"Stay out of our territory, and we won't," Talon warned.

He nodded once. "I have heard this and will abide by it."

Talon snorted. "Jesus, you've got some damn balls comin' here without anyone with you. Tell us what you think we stole and then this shit will be done."

"Mimi Takahashi."

"Mimi?" I said, and everyone looked at me. Mimi was a club girl. She and I had had a night together, but no more. "She's a club girl." Meaning he wouldn't get his hands on her.

Wolf snarled. "So she is here?"

"What do you want with her?" Talon asked.

"She's my sister."

"And?" Blue pressed.

A tick started at Wolf's temple. He breathed deeply through his nose, which seemed to help him compose himself. "Mimi disappeared. I have been looking for her. She needs to come home."

"When a woman becomes a part of the club, they're protected."

His upper lip rose. "She shouldn't have left in the first place."

"Why did she leave?" Griz asked. We wouldn't even bring her into this if she'd been treated badly in the first place.

"It is not what you're thinking," he said roughly.

"Then tell us, and we'll see if we bring Mimi out he —" Talon's words were cut off.

"Taro?" I tensed at the word sounding from behind me, ready to step in front of Mimi, but Talon held up his hand, halting me.

Wolf's whole body became taut at seeing his sister, his gaze shifting behind us. "Mimi." The single word was barely a whisper.

"What are you doing here?" Mimi stepped between Talon and Blue, her hands positioned protectively around herself.

"Finding you."

"I'm not coming back." Defiance lifted her words.

"Mimi—"

"No, Taro. I told them I refuse. I know it brings shame to the family, but I won't do it."

Wolf glanced around at us, obviously hesitant to speak in front of us, and I couldn't blame the guy. Obviously, it was a family issue.

"I have control over the family now, Mimi."

A small gasp escaped her as she cupped her throat. "Father?"

The clenching of Wolf's jaw was the only tell he gave, letting us know he didn't want to be discussing anything right now. "I would rather speak with you in private."

Mimi inhaled, the sound ragged, and she nodded.

"Come with me then." Wolf's gaze and tone softened.

"Ruin, you go with them," Talon ordered.

With pleasure. I'd have her back, even if she was

pissed at me for not taking up her offer for another hook-up.

Wolf's gaze hardened when he speared Talon with it. "She is family. She does not need a guard dog with her when with me."

"She's also been Hawks for six months. She's family to us, and she left your family for a reason. I won't have her goin' on her own."

"Mimi." Wolf's single word was clipped.

Mimi turned to Talon. "It's okay, Mr Marcus. I'm sorry I brought this trouble to your doorstep, but I will be safe with my brother." It did sound like she trusted her brother, but there was still a situation with her family.

Talon shook his head. "Mimi, girl, you've been here for a while. You know how this works. You walked into this compound and became a part of Hawks. No matter where you're goin' or what type of situation it is, we'll have your back. Take Ruin. He can stand away while you talk. But I'd feel better with a brother there."

Before Mimi could say anything, Wolf did. "Thank you for protecting her. Ruin is allowed to accompany us."

"Ruin?" Talon called.

"I'll follow behind," I said.

"Keep us posted." Talon hit me with a solid look, making his expectations clear.

"You got it, Prez," I replied and patted Coyote on the back before I moved off to my ride.

CHAPTER ONE

RUIN

*T*he situation was fucked.

I'd do anything for Mimi because she was a sweet woman. The problem was she just wasn't mine, and it made me feel like a heartless jackass since she'd made it clear she wanted me for more than just the one-night stand.

While we had our personal shit to deal with, I hoped it didn't mess with her other crap we were heading into. I followed Mimi and her brother as they drove to a nearby diner that was always open in the early hours. Once parked, I slipped off my ride and went inside after them.

Sitting a couple of booths away from them, I rested back and waited for the server to come and take my order. I needed a damn strong coffee to keep me going, and the day was just getting started. I hoped, with being far enough away but still in earshot, it would give Wolf a sense of comfort that I wasn't listening in, which I totally was.

"As I was saying in the car, Mimi, Father is on his deathbed. He wishes to see you, and you're telling me you do not want to come home?"

She winced and shook her head. "No, Taro."

"Mimi, I would not have come if I didn't believe I could take care of you."

"I know, brother, but you know what our uncles are like."

"They are not in charge. I am. They will listen to whatever I say. I will make sure of it."

"Taro, I trust you, I do. Leaving you has been the hardest decision in my life, but I knew you were strong, not like me. Women in our family aren't respected. We're ordered."

"I will change this."

She gave him a sad smile. "I hope you can, but it has been this way for decades."

The waitress approached them, and they asked for coffee. When she stopped at my table, I ordered two extra hot, double-strength coffees.

"Under my ruling, it will. Please, Mimi, come home with me this final time. I know you will regret this if you don't see him one last time."

"Taro...."

"Please. I will protect you. You could even bring him

along for extra security." He thumbed over his shoulder my way.

Her nose screwed up as she shook her head. Mimi drew in a deep breath. "Are you certain the uncles can't force this marriage on me?"

What the fuck?

"They won't. I will not allow it."

"My intended was fifty, Taro. *Fifty* to my nineteen years. Father was going to give me away to an old man for an alliance. Why would I want to see him?"

That was so messed up, I didn't even know what to think about it. Her father, the man who was supposed to take care of her, wanted her to marry an old fucker. I had a shit dad who beat my mum, but then Declan Stoke came into our lives, became my dad, and he was a man who loved with every fibre of his body. I goddamn looked up to him in many ways. He wouldn't stand for this shit if it was happening to anyone he knew. I wasn't going to either.

If Mimi was heading home, I'd go along for the ride and make sure no one screwed her over, since I didn't completely trust her brother. I'd feel better for having her back.

"Do it for you," Wolf said. "Tell Father exactly what you think. Be there for Mother. She will need you."

"She is the one who told me to run in the first place. If Father found out, he would have killed her."

"I wouldn't have allowed it. I have control over the family, the faction. I have my own people within the gang, ones who will only follow me, ones who I trust with my life and the lives of those I love. It will never be that way again. You and Mother will be taken care of. Things have changed. Trust me, Mimi, everything is better."

It had better be.

I gave a smile to the waitress when she dropped off my drinks before I pulled my phone out, placing it on the booth.

"Thank you," Mimi said to the waitress before she left and then looked back to her brother. "All right, Taro. I'll come back, but I will not stay long."

"I understand."

I shot a quick text to my club president, Talon.

Me: **Mimi's heading back to Melbourne. Her dad's on his deathbed. But shit at home don't look good. She ran because the dick dad tried to marry her off to a fifty-year-old dude for an alliance.**

Talon: **Fucking hell. You going with?**

Me: **Was thinking it. For added security. She still seems worried about her uncles trying to control her.**

Talon: **Yeah, go. Since the shit here has calmed, you'll have the time on your hands. If you run into any shit, have the brothers in Caroline Springs back you.**

Me: **You got it, boss.**

Talon: **Get back here and pack.**

Me: **On it.**

When I finished my second coffee, and they looked like they'd had enough chit-chat for one night, I stood and went to the counter to pay for all the coffees. They were just getting out of the booth when I turned and waited for them at the front door.

I tipped my chin up and said, "Talon has me on her security, so I'll be coming with you—"

"No!" Mimi snapped and glared up at me. She was cute when fiery. It was a damn shame I didn't see her as my one. I wished to Christ I did. She was stunning. I hated that I'd hurt her when I was an arsehole by telling her I didn't see us going further than that one night. I couldn't lie to her though. I couldn't have her thinking there was more between us.

I wanted what Stoke had with my mum.

What the prez had with his woman.

What Cody, my closest mate in the Hawks MC brotherhood, would soon have with bakery girl if he got his shit together.

I knew Mimi was pissed at me for the way I treated her, even though I'd been nice in the way I let her down. I wasn't going to walk away from helping her when she needed it.

Eventually she'd get over whatever she felt for me. *If* she still did feel something more than hatred for me.

I mean... I was a catch, but I knew, no, I *felt*, I honestly wasn't for Mimi. She had someone else waiting for her in the future.

Damn, I sound like a clairvoyant.

Raising my gaze to her brother, I lifted a brow, waiting to see if he had any objections. He nodded once. "I will allow this, for the club's sake, since you all have taken care of Mimi for so long."

"Thanks."

"No, I won't allow it. Ruin is…. He's annoying and… a pig."

"Harsh, babe, but true. I ain't the cleanest person when it comes to bedrooms." I grinned down at Mimi, who was still scowling, but I could feel Wolf's gaze burning into me. What was this guy thinking?

"Mimi, if this is what Talon wants, then allow him to come for his sake. We do not need the motorcycle club worrying." He knew I would have followed no matter because Talon had given me the go-ahead. It was good he knew not to mess with our club. Showed he was smart.

Mimi bit her bottom lip. She looked back to me. "Can't it be anyone but you? I'd even take Griz, and he scares me."

"Has he hurt you?" Wolf demanded.

When Mimi didn't answer right away, Wolf took it as a yes. He went to grab for me, but I dodged to the left, only I didn't see how fucking fast he was as he brought his leg up in a kick to the arm. I stumbled back into the wall, and his hand wrapped around my neck. I punched him in the gut. A noise escaped through his lips, but he didn't drop his hold. I went for the kidney. He blocked it with his knee and punched me in the fucking side.

"Stop," Mimi called. She pressed into her brother's side, holding his arm where his hand was still wrapped around my neck. Only it wasn't too tight, more holding me in place. "We…. Look, it was between Ruin and me, but it's fine." She stepped back with a small smile on her face. "Besides, I'm sure you've taught him a lesson."

"Have I?" Wolf asked darkly as he leaned into me.

"Sure." I smirked. If we weren't in a diner, I would have given him shit back and kept this going to see who would come out on top.

He moved away, dropping his hand, then walked out the front door. Mimi grinned at me as she swept by, following her brother.

She enjoyed seeing me get roughed up by her brother, even though I gave my own back, but honestly, I didn't give a shit. I deserved the beatdown for being a dickhead to her in the first place. Though, her brother had better not get an idea he could do it again. I'd have him on his back in seconds.

Jesus, I have to watch what I think, because that sounded sexual. I snorted internally at my choice of words. I supposed he was a good-looking guy, but fuck that, dudes just didn't do it for me.

Stepping out the door, I met them at the car. "We'll head back to the compound. Mimi and I can grab some shit, then we'll hit the road. That is, if you're not too tired, Wolf? Do you need a nap? That scuffle made you look ruffled. You need some beauty sleep?"

"It's nice of you to think I'm beautiful, but I'll be fine to drive."

I jerked my head back. "I did not call you beautiful," I insisted, incredulous.

"I think you did," Mimi added, looking to be having far too much fun.

"I so fuckin' didn't." Both smirked at me. "Christ, whatever. Let's just get there and on the damn road."

The sun was rising as I stalked off to my ride. Annoyance hissed through me, no doubt because of lack of sleep. At least the coffees I'd had would give me a nice buzz for a few hours, until I could get more in me.

I didn't have a clue what would happen in Melbourne. I just had to make sure I'd be alert. Already, I didn't like the sound of Mimi's family. The brother *seemed* okay, since he tried to kick my arse for his sister's honour, but I wasn't trusting him yet.

Even though I was heading into shit on my own, I had brothers, close friends in the Caroline Springs charter. I'd have help in a matter of moments should I need it.

Just sucked Coyote couldn't make the trip with me. But he had a store to run and a woman to claim. Other brothers would easily cover my shifts at the job site. I'd been working in construction since I turned eighteen and loved the hard work. Though, it'd be good to have some time off, since it'd been a while. But with no idea what my time off would involve, I couldn't wait to see exactly what I was up against.

CHAPTER TWO

RUIN

*T*he ride took over an hour. When we pulled up to a huge gated property and saw what was behind it, I couldn't believe my damn eyes. What type of fuckin' gang did Wolf control? By protecting Mimi, had I jumped right into more shit for the Hawks MC?

I shook my head and followed them through the gate after it opened. The prez wouldn't have allowed me to come in the first place if he didn't already know what type of crap Wolf was involved in. I trusted that.

A whistle slipped from my lips when I took in the mansion in front of me. Two people waited near the door, but you had to climb a shit ton of steps to get to them. I got off my bike after parking next to Wolf's car and removed my helmet. I didn't love leaving my Harley out in the elements. I'd have to see if there was a free spot in the massive ten-door garage at the end of the house. They couldn't have filled it with vehicles. Then again, as I took in more extravagant shit around me, I wouldn't be surprised.

With my saddlebag in hand, I stalked over to Wolf and asked, "Got a place for my ride in that garage?"

He nodded. "I'll have someone take it in if you'll give me the keys."

I stared at him. He had to be fucking kidding. No one touched my girl but me.

"He'll need someone to show him where to put it, but no one is to touch it but him," Mimi explained, and then she just had to add, "Bikers see their rides as their women. Well, a woman they would want to keep forever. Meaning they're very protective over them and would kill if any harm came to them."

It was true, but she could have said it without the dig.

"Very well." Wolf waved to the man waiting on top of the steps. He looked like he was in his sixties, but he jogged down those stairs like he was forty. "Katon will show you to the garage. Katon, Ruin is a guest. Please assist him in storing his ride inside."

"Yes, Taro-sama." Katon bowed at Wolf. It was obvious I'd arrived at a place set back in time with maids and butlers... or Mimi's family was so rich they probably wiped their arses with a five-hundred-dollar bill. "This way, sir," Katon said.

"Ruin. It's just Ruin."

"Of course." He bowed.

Wolf smirked and guided Mimi towards the front door. "We will see you inside."

I gave him a chin lift and followed Katon over to my bike. "Ah, Katon, no disrespect, but can we cut out the bowin'? I ain't used to it. Unless it's somethin' you were ordered to do, then go for it."

Katon's lips twitched, but he nodded and waited for me to set my bag back on my ride. I handed him my helmet while I steered my ride towards the garage.

"Guess the family has owned this place for a while?"

"Yes, sir—excuse me, Mr Ruin."

I sighed. "No mister, Katon. Just Ruin."

Katon smiled over at me. "To answer your question, the Takahashi family has owned this house for generations. It wasn't until fifteen years ago when it became their permanent residence instead of the one they have in Japan."

Yep, they were filthy rich.

"Have you been with them a while?"

"Ten years."

"That's a while."

"Taro-sama hired me. I am honoured to serve him." Taro, that was Wolf's real name. I'd heard Mimi use it.

Loyal. Got it. He wouldn't dish out any juicy details on his boss.

Still, I could find out a few things that weren't going

to give too much away, and he wouldn't feel guilty for it. "Is it only Wolf who lives here? And what's with that thing you say after using his name?"

"The whole Takahashi family does. Taro-sama's father and mother. Taro-sama's two uncles and their families. As well as trusted guards and workers, but they're situated in their own wing. Sama means leader or master. When Taro-sama took over, he offered the choice to call him Wolf or Taro-sama. I prefer the formal title."

Huh. Hoped Wolf wouldn't get his panties in a twist when I didn't call him master. "What types of businesses?"

His lips thinned. He pulled a device out of his pocket and pointed it at the garage. The doors slid open.

"They have many."

I had a feeling he wasn't pleased by some of them. I walked my ride into the garage and whistled at the large number of kickarse cars.

"Colour me impressed," I told Katon, who just smiled in return. We made our way back out, and Katon closed the door after us.

At the front door, Katon turned to me. "Please remove your shoes, and I will lay them in the cabinet near the door."

"What?"

"Your shoes, please remove them. We do not wear them in the house."

I slid my boots off, and Katon picked them up

before he opened the front door just as an intense voice hit me from the large entryway. "You bringing her here shames the family. She left, became a whore—"

"Whoa," I called out when I saw Mimi flinch. "Watch what you're fuckin' saying." I stopped beside an older guy standing in Wolf's face. Katon had made himself scarce. Shit, I probably should have done the same, but I didn't like the situation and wasn't running from it if I could stay and help.

"Who is this?" the man demanded as his judgemental gaze ran over me.

"Jiro Oji-san, this is Ruin, a friend of Mimi's and a guest of mine." Jiro, whoever the fuck he was to Wolf and Mimi, screwed up his face, and I knew a rant was about to come, but Wolf got in first. "You need to remember who is in charge of this family, Uncle. I will not have Mimi and my guest disrespected."

Jiro, their damn uncle, snarled, "It was the worst choice your father has ever made, leaving everything in your name. You will dishonour this family, and I won't stand by to watch it."

Wolf's hands clenched at his sides. "What are you saying, Uncle? Because the next thing out of your mouth had better be that you're leaving and taking your family with you. If you mean war between us, because I *will* fight, I will not back down and fold to your ways, then prepare to lose everything you love."

Holy fuck. Wolf wasn't messing around, and shit, the way he talked and stood up for Mimi had me wanting to have his back through it all. For Mimi's sake, I'd fight at his side.

The uncle ground his teeth together, glaring at Wolf. "We will see what the outcome is in the end."

Wolf's upper lip lifted when he growled out, "Yes, we will."

Jiro turned and stalked off, heading down a hall, and I had a feeling he wasn't going to back down anytime soon. What would be his next move though? I didn't trust Wolf, but my damn warning bells were ringing loudly when it came to the uncle.

"Taro, you shouldn't have done that," Mimi uttered.

"Bullshit," I commented.

They ignored me, and Wolf glanced down to his sister. "They have dominated our family for too long. Controlled in ways I would never. It's time to stop, and the sooner they realise I won't fold to their barbaric ways, the better."

"But, Taro, they're... lethal."

Wolf grinned, and if anything, it was a wolfish one. "So am I. I promised you that you had nothing to fear coming back, and I will honour my words." He tucked a strand of her black hair behind her ear. "Things will change."

"I fear for you."

He smirked. "You have nothing to worry about. I have protection, and you know I can take care of myself."

She nodded, frowning. "I know, but still, maybe it wouldn't have escalated if I hadn't come home."

Wolf cupped her cheeks and squished them together a little. Christ, it brought a smile to my face because it was something I'd do to my sister. "It was going to happen no matter what. I will not allow you to think this is your fault. It's not."

Mimi glared and pushed her brother's hands away. "I'll think how I want to."

Wolf smiled and curled his arm around her shoulders, moving them down the opposite hall to where the uncle headed. "Of course you will." He grunted after I heard a slap and then he laughed down at Mimi. "All I mean is that you're smart, Mimi. You got away. I should have, but now I'm neck-deep, and honestly, I wouldn't want it any other way, because I get to be the one to clean this family up."

I followed after them and thought they'd forgotten I was even there, so I said, "You two do know I'm still here, right?"

They both glanced over their shoulders. "You're like a pest I can't get rid of," Mimi said.

Wolf chuckled. "I would call him a pet, at least."

Narrowing my gaze, I shot them the middle finger. "I ain't either. I'm here as a favour. Now, feed the guest and show me to a damn room to crash in for a bit."

"Are pets always this demanding?" Wolf questioned his sister.

Mimi snorted. "I think it's only Ruin."

Clenching my jaw, I bit back my retort and let them have fun at my expense, since it looked like Mimi was enjoying herself and that was better than the pinched brows she'd had.

"Come, pet, I will feed you and bed you."

Mimi giggled while I choked on my own spit and started coughing.

Was Wolf gay?

Was he saying he wanted to take me to bed?

Women found me attractive, but men as well? Hell, my ego inflated over the knowledge. Not that I'd go there with a guy. Pussy was my thing, but it didn't mean I didn't like knowing men found me appealing too.

"Great, you've made his head swell even bigger now," Mimi said as we entered a kitchen.

"Hmm? How so?" Wolf asked, dropping his arm from around Mimi to move over to the refrigerator.

"He thinks you find him attractive and want to take him to bed."

That was an admission, right, that her brother was gay?

Wait, how did she read me so well? Christ, it was like my sister Nary's ability to read me. I never lied to her, because she'd sniff it out in seconds.

Laughter burst into the room, and I glared over at the culprit, crossing my arms over my chest.

Wolf wiped at his eyes and used his free hand to slap the bench. "Sorry." He chuckled. "I haven't laughed that long in a while." He grinned at his sister. "Is he really so vain?"

"I'm standing right here," I barked.

"Yes." Mimi nodded to Wolf.

"Hey, you don't know me enough to say that shit."

Mimi rolled her eyes. "Come on, all the girls know you love the attention when they fawn over you."

"I never remembered you being so outspoken before."

Mimi shrugged. "I've realised you're more like a brother to me, and I'm always real with Taro."

"I am not like a brother to you."

"What, is your ego taking a hit now you know I'm not attracted to you?"

I scoffed. Mimi was full of shit; she still found me hot. "You still like me."

They both stared at me, lips twitching.

Fuck me. I did sound vain. "Whatever." I glared.

Wolf started taking dishes out to lay them on the counter opposite from where I stood, with Mimi standing close. After I heard the door close and a throat clear, I looked up from the mouth-watering dishes and into Wolf's amused gaze.

I didn't want to ask, but I had to open my mouth. "What?"

"If it would make your ego better, I could bed you, even though you aren't my type."

I was everyone's type, dammit. I snorted. "Don't go doin' me any favours. Besides, I ain't into guys like that.... But, for curiosity's sake, what is your type?"

Of course, they laughed at my expense once more.

Groaning, I waved a hand in front of me. "Don't bother. I don't care, since I know I'm everyone's type. Can we just fuckin' eat?" I reached over and pulled a bowl close, wondering what in the fuck had I got myself into. Yeah, it was good Mimi was being herself around me and no longer seemed to want to throw daggers my way every second, and that she wasn't into me. But I wasn't sure I was going to survive their teasing or stop myself from looking like a self-centred, vain dickhead if we were here for another day or two.

CHAPTER THREE

RUIN

*W*hen I walked into the dining room for dinner, still with no shoes on, I paused. Wolf sat at the head of the table with a woman on his lap, draped over him. He smiled up at her like she was his first course.

Didn't he say he was gay?

Now I was just fucking confused. Hell, maybe he played both ways. If I had a thing for dudes, I'd do the same since it gave me more options of people to fuck. It was a smart decision on his part, really.

"Sir," Katon said from my side. He'd come to get me from my room, stating dinner was ready to be served. Wolf and Mimi had shown me to the room early, and I'd tried to get some shut-eye, but it hadn't worked.

Instead, I'd jacked off in the shower, then called a few people to catch up.

Rolling my eyes, I asked, "What'd I say, Katon?"

His smile was small. "Ruin, if you would head to the end of the table and sit beside Taro-sama, I will let the servers know everyone is here."

I actually didn't want to sit down at the damn table, since there were twenty-odd too many people for my liking. If this was what family dinners were like here, I didn't want to be a part of it, but I was damn starved once more.

"Got it." I made my way down the long-arse table. Seriously where did they get a table so big?

When I'd entered, I'd caught the attention of most at the table. Some stared, others whispered behind their hands, and a few looked at me like I was dirt. Uncle Jiro was one of them, of course.

Even Mimi was watching me as I took my seat opposite her and beside Wolf at the head. She gave me a tentative smile, and I could read how uncomfortable she was sitting there by her posture.

I gave her a chin lift. "What's happenin'?"

Someone down the table snorted. I swear all these people couldn't be their whole family. When I said it was about twenty-odd too many, I meant it. I'd be happy just sharing dinner with Mimi and Wolf. The others all peered around, judging everyone, even from within their family. Right then, Jiro's glare was transferred from me to someone across from him, another man a few years older than Wolf.

I pulled my gaze back to Mimi and tried again, "You good?"

She nodded, and a small "Yes," dropped from her mouth. I didn't like seeing her like this. She'd been smiling, laughing, and seemed at ease just that afternoon, and now she was like a rabbit waiting for the fox to bite.

I shifted my gaze to Wolf, which he met before he glanced to Mimi with thinned lips. Yeah, he didn't like it either. So why in the fuck was he giving the bitch on his lap all the attention and not easing Mimi's tension?

"Get rid of her," I ordered quietly.

Wolf's gaze flashed back to me, and even the woman lifted her head from his shoulder to glare at me.

Wolf's nostrils flared. He didn't like me ordering him, but he was being a dick to Mimi, and I didn't like that. Still, with his hands on the woman's waist, he moved her to her feet and took her hand, kissing the back of it. "I'll see you later, my lovely."

She smiled coyly, but it was too late. We all knew she was just a slut looking for a banging. "In your room?"

"Of course."

She rested her free hand on his shoulder and brushed it down his arm as she turned. After shooting me daggers again, she finally left the room. I didn't give a shit that I'd pissed her off.

Wolf picked up a knife and twirled it around his fingers. He rested his elbows on the table and leaned my way. "Never speak to me like that again."

My lips tipped up, and I chuckled low. I leaned close also. "Your sister's back for the first night, yet you sit there with some bird on your lap ignoring the glares she's getting—"

"Ruin," Mimi snapped low and shook her head.

Wolf flicked the knife my way, holding it with the tip of the blade to my neck. "What goes on at this table or in the house is how *I* want it. You're here because *I* allow it. That can change if you piss me off again." He placed the knife back down, smiled at the people around the table, and clapped his hand before he took Mimi's hand and squeezed it.

Mimi smiled up at him.

Fuck.

Maybe I'd jumped to the wrong conclusion, and I'd missed something.

Doors opened, platters were brought forward and set down throughout the table. No one moved to grab their food though.

Wolf cleared his throat. "Tonight, we welcome back my sister, Mimi, and with her is our guest, Ruin. I want no harm to come to either of them. If something happens, the person responsible will be punished."

What the fuck? Seriously, I didn't think Wolf ran the whole house like Talon did the Hawks MC, but they all sat there listening to him like the brotherhood listened to Talon. Some looked peeved over the idea of not harming us, but the others nodded and accepted his order.

I thought that'd be it, that we could eat and get out

of there, especially for Mimi's sake, but of course it wasn't.

Jiro stood. "I will not eat at this table with people who desert the family and dishonour us." His hard gaze landed on Mimi.

A look of anger swept over Mimi, and she stood. Her chair screeched over the hardwood floor. All eyes were on her when she said, "I would not have dishonoured the family if one of you had listened to me when I said I would not marry *that* man."

"It was a promised business deal. You have no right to tell us how to run things. You listen and do as you're told."

I snorted. I couldn't help it. "How fuckin' outdated." I grunted when a foot met with my shin.

Wolf glowered at me before he stood and rested his hands on the table, staring down the room. "Since my father has signed everything over to me, you have noticed some things have changed already. More changes will come. Within the family and businesses."

Another man stood quickly. "It is not something we speak of in front of outsiders." Gazes turned on me and Mimi. Christ, I couldn't fucking believe Mimi was seen as an outsider for not marrying an old fucker.

"I did not say I would speak of all changes now. The businesses are for another day, but for the family, that is another matter. I want to touch on one subject only. No longer will the women of the family be bargained off in any type of deals. They will not be forced into an arranged marriage *unless* they are willing and I hear it from them myself."

"This is not how it's done," Jiro boomed.

Goddamn old prick.

Wolf straightened. "It is now, on my word."

"Come," Jiro ordered two women and three men, all of different ages, beside him. If I had to guess, one woman was his wife, the other his mother. The men looked younger, maybe his sons. Jiro stopped, and when he did, the rest of his family halted and looked down at two girls in their late teens. "Yuri, Hina, now."

They bowed their heads and stared at their plates.

"Ima oki nasai, on'nanoko," the wife snapped in Japanese.

I saw the older teen take the younger's hand. "W-We don't want to marry the men you have us set with."

Jesus Christ. They were younger than Mimi and already had been set to marry someone. That was fucked up. I wanted to wrap my hands around Jiro's neck and choke the life out of him.

"You are my daughters. You will follow my rule!" Jiro yelled.

I stood, ready to storm around the table and lay the fucker out. A hand dropped to my shoulder. Wolf's. He didn't say anything to me. When he removed his hand, he moved closer to Jiro and said to the room, "From this day on, the women have their say on how *their* lives are lived." He stopped just before Jiro. "That is my word."

"They are my children."

"They are a part of the Takahashi family." Wolf cocked his head to the side. "Tell me, Oji-san, who runs the family?"

Jiro's jaw clenched, along with his fists. "You." It was pretty clear he left off "for now." Calculating intent filled his eyes. I expected he wouldn't even flinch from killing his own nephew—as long as he had control in the end.

Mimi's life wasn't the only one in jeopardy within these damn walls. Wolf's was as well.

I hadn't, as yet, seen the muscle backing Wolf. Would he have enough protection? Would they both? I'd stick around and stay close to see. If not, I would make sure they did by calling the brothers in.

"Yuri, Hina, come," Jiro tried again. If they left, I worried for their safety. I wouldn't put it past Jiro to beat them bloody for "dishonouring" him in front of the rest of the family.

The girls looked to Wolf. He smiled gently. "If you wish to move to this side of the property, I am sure your aunt will love the company."

"You will not take them!" the mother yelled.

I caught Mimi wrapping her arms around her waist and biting her bottom lip. I quickly moved around the table and rested my hands on her shoulders in support. She leaned back into my chest.

Wolf's gaze hardened and swung to the woman. "The girls will still be within the walls, just closer to me so I know my ruling will be followed." Yeah, Wolf also

33

knew the girls were going to get in the shit for speaking up.

Jiro's face shot red as he screwed it up. He took two steps back and grabbed Yuri's hair. She cried out as he pulled her from her seat. Hina started crying. She dropped to her knees and pressed her forehead to the floor by her father's feet.

"They are not your problem. I am their father. They will do what *I* say." He shook Yuri by the hair, a whimper falling from her lips.

Fuck this.

I started around Mimi, but she gripped my arm. "No," she uttered. "Taro will take care of it." I took another step. "Please, Ruin. It's a family matter. You can't get involved unless asked by the head of the family. *Please.*"

I didn't like it one damn bit. But I locked my body down and glanced back to see the men had joined Jiro at his back. All of them scowled at the girls like they were a disease.

"You do not want to do this," Wolf warned as he removed his white jacket.

"You have no say over *my* children," Jiro snarled.

"I have a say over the treatment of any member of this family, and I do not like what I see. Let Yuri go, Jiro."

"You will call me Oji-san, boy."

Wolf chuckled without humour. "You do not deserve the title when I have no respect for you."

Jiro's face screwed up again and he pushed Yuri

away. She stumbled and dropped to her butt. In the next second, Jiro raised his hand and slapped Wolf across the face. A bit of a bitch move, but maybe it was something this family did.

Wolf slowly moved his gaze back to Jiro. "You want to do this now?"

"I will never bow to you as head of the family." He turned to the room and waved a hand at Wolf. "This is who you will follow? This pup? He is still wet behind his ears. He knows nothing. He will change everything, and you will sit there letting him? He sucks cock, he takes men to bed, and soon you will be bending over for him."

Jesus Christ.

Another man stood abruptly. "I will not follow a man who takes other men."

Bloody hell, were they all bigots?

"My personal life has nothing to do with how I run the business or the family. No matter who I take to bed."

"You ask us to change from the old ways, and you're not willing to change?" the man asked.

"Akio Oji-san, the changes I make will never affect the businesses. And doing it without forcing the women of the Takahashi family to do things they never should have to do. Our own father knew of the changes I would make, and yet he still picked me. This was even before he was as close to death as he is now. Maybe having his daughter run from our lives over a business deal where she had to marry an old man had him seeing things in a new light."

"Never," Jiro yelled. "It was you getting in his head. Everything ran smoothly in our lives until now, until you."

Wolf scoffed. "Smoothly? It's so smooth your daughters quiver at your feet because they do not wish to marry men older than them, men who abuse women. Do you not care for their welfare?"

This family was screwed up. Everything just angered me to a point my gut burned. The old cunts needed to back down and let Wolf take charge. I could see he would be a good leader, and I wasn't the only one reading some of the respectful gazes sent his way. He fought for the women, and I knew he'd fight for others who came to him for help against old-fashioned crap.

Wolf snorted. "Of course you do not care when you are also one who lays your hands on them."

"Enough," Jiro belted out.

"Never. I will protect them and anyone who needs it in the family. Even if it's from their own father." He crossed his arms over his chest. "You have no choice here, Jiro, because I run things in the Takahashi family, and that is my final word." He turned his back on Jiro. I wasn't sure it was wise. "Mimi, come get the girls and take them to your room." Mimi started forward, but I wasn't letting her go alone. I matched her pace. While Mimi helped Yuri stand, I tucked my hands under Hina's arms and brought her to her feet.

Jiro made a noise in the back of his throat, and I

caught the nod he sent just before the three men at his back advanced towards Wolf.

"Wolf," I barked, since he hadn't seemed to have seen them.

However, as soon as they were close, Wolf struck one in the throat, one in the chest, the other in the kidney. They tried to fight back, but Wolf counteracted it with a quick punch or kick. Never had I seen anyone move as fast as he did. His movements flowed, his body twisted and bent. In moments, the three men were on the floor, groaning and clutching some part of their bodies.

"Leave," Wolf ordered Jiro.

Jiro waited for a couple of moments, glowering at Wolf before he snapped at the older women, and they walked out the room.

"Ryo," Wolf called loudly.

A door opened, and five men dressed in black walked in. They had damn swords strapped to their hips, but I also saw guns strapped to their other side. The one in front, who I guessed was Ryo, stopped and bowed to Wolf.

He nodded towards the men on the floor. "Take them out of here."

Ryo clipped, "Sorera o shita ni motte itte kudasai." The others behind him moved forward and collected the fools on the ground, taking them from the room. When they were out of earshot, Ryo added to Wolf, "Next time, do not ask me to wait out in the hall. I am here to protect you."

Wolf grinned. "You know I had it handled."

"It does not matter."

"I'm sure there'll be other situations."

Ryo huffed and crossed his arms over his chest. Was he pissed he didn't get in on the action? Probably. The two of them seemed close. Then again, they must have been for Ryo to speak to Wolf like that. I doubted Wolf would accept that attitude from many.

Wolf patted Ryo on the arm and addressed the room. "Anyone else wish to go against my new rule?"

Silence.

The other older guy had even sat down.

"Then let's eat." He faced Ryo again. "Ryo, could you take over from Mimi and get the girls to Okaa-san?"

Ryo nodded and gently wound an arm around Hina's waist, taking her from my hold. Then he did the same for Yuri. Wolf got close to them, cupping a cheek on each girl. They lifted their gazes to his.

"You have my protection. You have my love. I will make sure you never have to do anything you wish not to." They clasped his hand in each of theirs and bowed, pressing their foreheads to the back of his hands.

"Thank you, Jiā jūn, thank you."

I leaned into Mimi and asked, "What's that word mean?"

"Jiā jūn?"

"Yeah."

"Head of house."

"Rise, girls, and go with Ryo. I'll have Katon bring you something to eat soon. Do not fear for anything."

They bowed a couple more times and went with Ryo. Wolf moved to Mimi and me. I jolted a little when his hand landed on my waist. "Let's eat," he said. I turned back to the table and felt his hand slide to my lower back, guiding his sister and me back to our seats.

It was damn weird having a guy's hand on my back, but I wasn't going to make a fuss about it in front of everyone. Obviously, there were many rules and traditions in the house, and I knew I'd stuff up over something, probably kicking someone's arse, but for now, I'd keep my mouth shut.

Respect for the guy who just pulled out my seat ran through me, despite my brows shooting high, wondering why the fuck he made such a gesture. If we had more time here, I could even come to like the man. That was if he stopped treating me like some woman, since he'd just tried to place a napkin on my lap.

I snatched it out of his hand and glared up at him. The prick smirked.

Maybe liking him as a person was not going to last long. I had a feeling he'd get on my nerves more than anything.

CHAPTER FOUR

RUIN

*A*fter dinner, Mimi and I stood in a library. I'd pulled her aside to see how she was, since she'd gone to see her father earlier. Pouring us a drink, her hands shook a little. I placed my palms on her shoulders. "Let me do that, babe."

She handed me the bottle of bourbon and took the glass she'd already poured, stepping out of the way. After I got myself a couple of licks of straight Kentucky, I turned and leaned against the bar and watched her pace in front of me.

"I'm guessin' it didn't go well."

She sucked back her drink and faced me. "He was sleeping when I went."

"You didn't get to speak with him then."

Mimi rolled her eyes. "I suppose I could have talked to him while he slept." I took on her irritation. She'd come here for one thing, and that was to sort shit out with her father before he kicked the bucket. Since it hadn't happened, she was probably fretting over the thought. Her shoulders sagged. "Sorry."

"It's all good, honey. I get it."

Mimi grazed her bottom lip with her top teeth. Usually that move would get my dick paying attention, but he was asleep. It proved Mimi wasn't my one. God, it sucked, because I wanted to find her, and Mimi was a great woman. But honestly, now wasn't the right time to be thinking any of this shit.

A change of subject was what was needed. "You've got a lot of people in the family."

She laughed. "Yes, you could say that. Some still live in Japan. They refuse to…. Well, I guess they don't like Australia or the US, where our other uncle resides over the Takahashi family that moved there."

"What's so different from there to here?"

"Everything. In Japan, they're stricter than here."

"Fuck."

"Exactly. In a way, it was good Dad moved us here. Although, he was still strict. More with Taro since he is the family's heir. If Taro ever spoke out of turn, he was punished." Her lips thinned. "Really, I had the better end of the deal."

"Doesn't mean your turmoil is any less than his, Mimi. You were gonna be sold off like an item instead of a person."

Mimi poured herself another drink. "Right. Some still do that in Japan. The main difference from here to there is how different the houses are. Traditionally, we should live in wooden houses with mat flooring and sliding doors. Rooms are divided by partitions of paper. Which makes things awkward when you can hear things going on in the other room."

"You would have been young when you lived there, yeah?"

"I was, but Mother always went back to see her family and took Taro and me with her."

"How is your mum?"

Mimi shrugged. "I haven't seen her yet."

I dipped my brows, confused over why that wouldn't have been the first thing she'd done. They'd been close, right? Hell, if I hadn't been home in ages, I'd head straight to my mum.

"How come?"

"I didn't want to interrupt her praying." She took a sip of her drink and whispered, "I worry she won't want to see me."

"Babe. She will. You're a cool chick. I'm sure your mum has missed you."

She smiled softly. "A cool chick?"

"Yeah."

I glanced down at her hands as she wrapped them around her glass and sucked in a deep breath. "I'm sorry for how I acted after...."

"It's fine, honey."

She shook her head. "It wasn't. I didn't know what it

was back then, but I have a feeling now that I looked to you for comfort and... I didn't want to lose that after we'd slept together, because I worried I wouldn't keep that comfort if we didn't keep sleeping together. I also realised recently it was more leaving the compound that I worried about. I felt safe there."

"You'll always be a part of Hawks, babe. Even if you don't sleep with any members. Hell, Mouth could get you a job in there cleaning or working the bar to pay for your room. Never think we'd kick you out because you don't have one of our cocks between your legs."

A blush hit her cheeks. "You and... Cowboy were the only ones I'd slept with."

"Cowboy, hey?"

The blush deepened. Shit, if I had to guess, someone had a crush.

"Yes." She shook her head. "Anyway, I also wanted to thank you for coming here with me. I didn't think it could be like this between us."

"It's nice. Now that you don't hate me."

She laughed. "Yes. Though, I never hated you. You annoyed me, a lot, with your cocky ways, but more in a brother way."

"Babe," I drew out. "Never call me a brother, since we fucked."

I drew another laugh from her. "You're right. If anyone heard, it would be weird." She rested her hand on my arm and looked up at me, suddenly serious. "Honestly, I must thank you for coming. Having you here... it helps knowing I'm not alone in this." She shook her head. "I know I have my brother and mother here, but it's been so long since I've seen them, and Hawks has become a part of my life."

I placed my hand over hers. "We're your family also, Mimi. Always."

She smiled softly up at me.

"Say, can you tell me what that situation was with the woman hangin' all over Wolf? I had a feelin' I missed somethin'."

"You did. He only had her there to distract the family from my arrival."

Shit. "Then I fucked it up."

Mimi shook her head. "You didn't. He would have sent her on her way in the end anyway."

"Back to his room. I thought your brother was gay."

"She's an old friend of Taro's and would have known to leave and not enter his room. Taro's only into men. But if Taro had a man draped over him, a war would have started."

I snorted. "Yeah, I could see that happenin'."

Bigoted fucks.

"Am I interrupting something?"

We jolted apart like we'd been caught making out by our parents. Only it was Wolf standing in the library doorway, glaring at us.

"No, you're not," Mimi said with a grin. "Come join us for a drink, *aniki*."

His eyes softened. "Of course." He stepped into the room and made his way over to the bar. His gaze dropped to Mimi's hand on my arm and how mine still covered hers. Was he worried his sister and I would start things back up again, and he didn't like it?

Wolf curled his arm across Mimi's chest and pulled her back into his arms, kissing her temple. "It is good to see you in this house again, *shisutā*."

Her hands lifted to grip his arm. "It's good to be here, with you."

"What's that you call each other?"

"Aniki and shisutā?" Wolf asked.

"Yeah."

"Brother and sister."

I nodded. "Sounds cool when you say it."

"Who, me or my sister?" Wolf asked, a smirk playing on his lips.

Rolling my eyes, I replied, "Never mind."

"What about if I speak to you in Japanese, will it turn you on?"

I snorted. "No. Again, I ain't into guys."

Mimi slapped her brother's arm. "Stop teasing."

"Shikashi watashi wa sore ga sukidesu."

I didn't know what he said, and I'd never admit it to him, but it sounded good. Instead, I kept his gaze and took a sip of my drink.

Wolf laughed as he nodded to my glass. "Can I have a sip?"

I scowled. "Get your own."

"But your mouth hasn't been on any of those."

What the fuck?

"Shall I leave the two of you alone?" Mimi asked teasingly.

"No," I blurted.

"Yes," Wolf said.

"No," I clipped.

"Yes. I could go all night. Just ask me." Wolf winked.

"Can we go back to when you were threatening me?" I suggested. It was easier then. I didn't know if he found me attractive and wanted me. Because seriously, the guy flirted like it was his own language. If I was into guys, his flirting could have worked; instead, it just twisted my gut, since he wasn't getting the hint I wasn't into it.

I didn't do dicks. I liked sliding into warm, tight wetness.

That's what arseholes are for. With added lube.

Jesus, shut up, brain.

Yes, anal was good, but a vag was better because along with it, there were curves, breasts, hair. Okay, the dude before me had hair. Long, dark hair that was draped around his shoulders. When did he take it out from the tie?

Nope. I didn't care. Where the fuck was I going with that thought?

Wolf kissed Mimi's temple again and moved to make himself a drink. "If you like threats, Ruin, I can give you some."

Shit, where was he going with this? My gut twisted again.

He smirked. "Depends how kinky you are—"

Groaning, I announced, "I'm out." I put my glass on

the bar, making my way towards the door. Both those fuckers behind me laughed.

"I'm only teasing, Ruin. Come back."

I shook my head. "Nope. I need sleep anyway." As soon as I said it, I winced.

"Is that an invite?" Wolf asked.

I shot the middle finger over my shoulder.

"Very well, I get the hint. Mimi dear, Mother has been asking for you."

I stopped at the door and looked back. I caught Mimi's gaze. "You good?"

She smiled and nodded. "I am, thanks. Get some rest. Wolf will go with me."

"I will."

I gave them a chin lift and walked out the library before Wolf could say anything more.

When I'd first met him, he'd seemed closed off, cold. I never would have expected a goddamn flirt lay underneath. The things he'd said... Christ, I didn't know how to take them, and you'd think I would, since I was brought up around Julian.

Julian was an over-the-top flamboyant gay man related to the Marcus family by being Zara's brother's man. The things that would come out of his mouth were surprising but fucking funny. Especially when he'd give the old brothers in the club hell. He meant nothing by it, because he was completely devoted to Mattie, and they had a daughter together. So maybe Wolf was like Julian, though not as flamboyant, but all talk and no action, meaning he didn't mean anything he said to me.

Yeah, that was it.

He was just messing with me.

Hell, I could let the flirting happen and think nothing of it. If only my gut would quit twisting in a way I didn't understand every time he said something or looked at me with interest. Shit, was I a homophobic prick? Well, not in general, because I didn't care where people got their love from, as long as they were happy. Like Beast and Knife, Julian and Mattie. Even Pick and Billy who were with Josie; but was my gut reacting in a way where it didn't like what Wolf was doing?

Scrubbing a hand over my face, I groaned because I didn't have a fucking clue.

Guess I'd see with time.

Then again, we may not be around for much longer, so I wouldn't see Wolf again. Probably for the best. The guy was all right enough, ran his family well, but there was still something about him I wasn't sure about.

His dark eyes flashed into my mind. Was that it? Something in them I didn't trust?

Opening the door to my bedroom, I beelined for the bed and stripped out of my clothes. I needed sleep, desperately. Maybe my head would be clearer in the morning, and Wolf's ways wouldn't get to me so much.

CHAPTER FIVE

RUIN

*E*arly in the morning a few days later, I stood outside the door to the master suite. Mimi had been woken to see her father while he was lucid. If I had my way, I wouldn't be there, but Mimi had barged into my room and asked me to come along, to wait until she spoke with him. She needed support, and I would give it to her. I'd give her anything she asked for because I'd come to care for her like a sister. Wolf was with her, along with their mother. She had her family at her back, but I could understand wanting more from me. If I was in her situation, I'd want a person around who I was used to.

Since I'd fucked up, we weren't that close, but I was

her comfort blanket from home, and she did see Ballarat as her home. I knew that much.

Voices rose from behind the closed door, and I fisted my hands when I heard roared, "You disgust me. You are no child of mine."

Fuck.

Other voices intervened, and the tone went lower where I couldn't hear what was being said. Still, I wanted to march in there and tell this fucker to stop being a bitch to his own daughter. Mimi didn't need this. Not the hate when all she wanted to do was reconcile things before he died.

I caught the guards' gazes from across the hallway. Five of them. Ryo, who waited for Wolf as his personal guard, another one was there to watch over the dad, and two waited for Wolf's mum and Mimi. The last I'd seen around a lot when I'd wandered around the place because he'd been not far behind me every time I moved out of my room. When I asked about the guard on the walk to the room, Wolf informed me that Botan was my personal guard while I stayed under his roof.

Through clenched teeth, I'd informed him, "I can take care of myself."

Wolf had winked and said, "He's there as a just-in-case scenario. I wouldn't want anything to happen to you from someone on my side."

"Again, I can take care of myself."

When his gaze scanned my body, my gut had twisted. Wolf then smirked. "I know." And that was all he said before we stopped outside the suite and they went in.

Botan stared back now, and I wanted to ask him if he was there to protect me—*scoff*—or to keep an eye on me because they didn't trust me. If it was the second thing, I couldn't blame him. I was a stranger in their house at a time when even I wouldn't want an outsider around. Although, if it was because he didn't trust me, why not just say it instead of implying I couldn't take care of myself?

Fuck me.

I was overthinking again.

Whatever it was, I couldn't complain because it wasn't my place. I was there for Mimi, to protect her, and I really wanted to protect her against her father as his voice rose once again with more harsh words.

When I turned towards the door, Ryo called, "Don't."

Facing him, I crossed my arms over my chest. "Why the fuck not?" I waved a hand at the door. "He's cutting her with each fuckin' word. I'm here to protect her, even from shit like that."

It was then Wolf's voice rose from within the suite. "Silence. If this is the last time you speak with your own daughter, is this how you want her to remember you? A heartless bastard ruled by work?"

"That is why," Ryo said. "You are an outsider. Walking in there would have been the worst you could have done for Mimi. You don't know him enough, but

Wolf will protect his sister, even from her father and his words."

"He took his damn time," I grumbled because I didn't want to see Wolf as a good guy.

"He knows when to intervene. He did not rule this family because of inheritance. Even his father saw how cutthroat he could be. He plays it smart when needed."

"He is a good sama," Botan commented with a glare my way.

The doors behind me opened with a rush, and in the next second, I had a crying woman in my arms.

"Fuck, babe. You're okay. I got you."

Mimi's whole body shook as she gripped the back of my tee. I lifted my gaze as an older version of Mimi stepped through the doors before Wolf closed them with him still inside. His gaze hard, his jaw clenched. My guess, he'd be having more words with his father.

"I t-tried to get him to understand." She sobbed into my chest. With a hand to her waist, I rested my other one at the back of her head, gently holding her to me.

"Understand what?"

"T-That the man h-he bargained me with sold his women to other men to use. T-That he b-beat them."

Christ. Motherfucking Christ. The fucker still didn't listen to reason about why she ran, even after knowing what would have happened to his own daughter if they went ahead with the trade.

Anger boiled my blood. My body twitched. I wanted to go in there and end his life for him, in a bloody mess.

"*Musume*," the mum uttered, resting her hands on

Mimi's shoulders. Mimi turned abruptly and pushed her face into her mum's shoulder. "My sweet girl, let's go to your room." I caught Mimi nod into her shoulder. "Ryo?"

"Your guards will follow. I'll inform Wolf when he's out."

"Mimi?" I asked, not sure if I followed or not.

Mimi lifted her face, tears streaming down her cheeks. "I'll see you soon?"

It meant she wanted time with her mum, and I completely understood. I nodded. "You got it."

They started down the hall, and I faced Ryo. With a snarl, I asked, "There a gym in here?"

"Botan will show you."

Good. I needed to work off some of this aggression, or I would go in that room and kill the cunt. I didn't give a shit that he was dying already. Not when he was breaking Mimi's heart all over again.

MY GUT GRUMBLED AGAIN. I rubbed at it as I walked into the kitchen, having missed breakfast. I was happy to help myself, because I'd needed that workout and a shower more than food.

Botan stepped into the kitchen when I got to the refrigerator and opened it.

"Want anythin'?"

"No."

It was fine with me, since the guy annoyed me for

even being there in the first place. Guess I could stop being polite. I pulled out leftovers and found a plate after searching through too many damn cupboards, all without the help of Botan. I didn't have a clue what the foods were, but they smelled fantastic, and as soon as I got it heated and in my mouth, my gut thanked me.

I stood at the sink, eyes out the window to the overcast day, and wondered if Mimi could use a day out instead of sticking around here. I knew I could, and I'd been meaning to go to the Caroline Springs charter since arriving.

I'd been in contact with brothers from the charter, and all kept asking when I was going to drop in. Could be a good distraction for Mimi this afternoon.

Hands at my waist had me dropping the plate to the counter with a clatter, jumping around, and hitting my arse against the counter. Wolf's eyes lit with humour as he took a step forward. I glanced over his shoulder as my gut twisted.

"I sent him away," Wolf said softly, and before I could react, his body heat rested against my front, his hands back on my waist, and his lips moved to my neck where he kissed.

I froze.

Fucking froze except for my eyes shooting wide. "What are you doin'?"

I *felt* his lips smile against my skin. "Giving you a good morning kiss."

Pressing my hands to his shoulders, I shoved him back. "Fuck off," I clipped, screwing my nose up.

Wolf straightened, lips thinned, and he took a step back while he studied me. I knew he'd see my chest rising and falling rapidly, but it was because he'd scared the hell out of me—the silent ninja prick.

It had nothing to do with my skin still burning where his lips had been.

Nothing.

Wolf's expression blanked, and he walked to the coffee machine. "Relax, Ruin. I was messing with you."

I didn't know what to say, because now I felt like a prick for telling him to fuck off. The blank expression didn't sit well with me, which was strange. Why did I care? I didn't know the guy. Yet even when it didn't sit well, I couldn't bring myself to say or do anything for his coldness to stop.

He didn't say anything more either. I picked up my plate, finished the food on it, and watched as he made his coffee. He then walked out of the room without saying another word.

Botan stood in the kitchen doorway in the next moment, and there was an extra edge to his glare at me.

I returned it because I hadn't done anything wrong. Wolf had scared me, I'd reacted, but who gave the guy the right to do that in the first place? I'd said I wasn't into guys, yet there was Wolf all up in my grill, touching me, *kissing* my skin, like I was something to him.

That was... wrong.

I wasn't anything to him.

I didn't want to be anything to him.

So why did I feel like I'd disappointed him somehow?

Snorting to myself, I rinsed the plate and placed it in the dishwasher. It didn't matter if I disappointed Wolf or not. I didn't care.

My gut twisted again as I rubbed at my neck, my gaze lifting to the window just as the rain started pouring. Suddenly, I wasn't in the mood to go see the brothers.

The sooner I got out of this place, though, the better. Stuffing my hands in my pockets, I left the kitchen and made my way to Mimi's room. I knocked once. If her mum was still in there, I would leave.

The door opened, and Mimi gave me a small smile. "Hi." She opened the door further, and I walked in. When she closed the door, I pulled her into a hug and caught her drawing in a shuddering breath.

"Hey." I yelped when she pinched my side. "What was that for?"

"Why couldn't you have been like this back when we—"

"Because I was a dickhead."

"And because we aren't *it* for each other."

Sighing, I rested my chin on the top of her head. "Yeah."

Mimi hugged me tightly. "I'm glad you're here though."

"So am I." Because if I wasn't here, I wouldn't have had the chance to get to know Mimi for who she actually was, and even though she wasn't my one, I wanted to have her in my life. "You doin' okay?"

With a shrug, she moved over to the bed, sitting in the middle of it, crossing her legs. She patted a spot, and I sat near her, leaning back against the headboard.

Mimi's gaze stayed on her crossed legs while she played with the hem of her oversized tee. "It's hard being here," she admitted.

"It would be. Your dad's a dick."

She gave me a small giggle, exactly what I was trying for. "He is."

"What do you wanna do, babe? No pressure. I'm here for you, to have your back. I'll go when you do."

Her hand shot out and clasped mine. "Thank you."

"No need for thanks, honey."

She shrugged with a smile. "I... I need to think about what I want to do."

"Take all the time you need, Mimi."

She nodded. "Taro's throwing a party for Ryo's birthday soon. He's asked me to go."

Taro.

Never really took in his name before.

And I don't need to now either.

"I'll go if you want to."

"I'll see," she said softly.

"No problem." Mimi went back to staring down at her legs, lost in thought again. "Hey, how about we head to that huge-arse theatre room and watch some movies?"

A small smile touched her lips. "That sounds good, actually."

"Cool." We moved off the bed and headed for the door. I wasn't sure if I was offering a day of movies for a distraction just for Mimi though. I reckoned I needed it also.

Because of him.

Which was damn weird.

CHAPTER SIX

RUIN

"*Giving you a good morning kiss.*"

Opening my eyes, I cursed repeatedly and even hit the bed with my fists a couple of times. Those damn words had been waking me up since Wolf had said them over a week ago. It pissed me off. I didn't get why my mind was stuck on those words, since it was obvious Wolf had been, like he said, messing with me at the time.

However, he'd stopped his teasing after that incident.

Of course, I was glad he had, but in doing so, he'd become more aloof with me. If we were in the same room together, he'd nod in greeting but wouldn't talk to me. While I didn't understand the cold change, it was for the best.

It was.

Yawning, I pressed a hand over my mouth and... morning breath. A thump against the wall that connected to Wolf's room had me sitting up. I was ready to see if there was anything wrong, but nothing else happened after the first noise.

I could easily go back to sleep since I didn't get much the night before. I'd been in Mimi's room comforting her since, once again, she'd been distraught over her father and his shit words when she'd tried to reason with him.

The guy needed to die already. It was cold, but damn true. The longer the mean bastard lingered, the more hurt it brought Mimi, his words festering in her mind.

It fucking gutted me to see her in a state where she couldn't stop crying and found it hard to breathe. Eventually, last night, her mum had come to take care of her and had asked me to leave. I didn't until Mimi gave me the go-ahead.

Christ, I knew there were people out there with shit parents and families. My real father had been one. He was a long-gone memory, though, as Nary and I had Stoke in our lives. He'd shown us how important we were to him by taking us on. Not only that, but by looking after and loving our mum. When they'd had a kid together, a sister for us who was now nine, I thought things would change and Stoke would be different to us since we weren't his biological kids. Especially since Nary and I were older. But they hadn't.

We were just as important to him as Rayne was.

I was damn lucky to have my family. Mum had never been as happy as she was with Stoke. Nary had her own happily ever after with Vicious, after her nightmare situation, and Vicious had stepped up to claim his woman after they'd been dancing around each other for years.

It was my turn to find mine. It wouldn't be anytime soon, though, since I didn't have that connection Mum had with Stoke or Nary had with Vicious.

I hoped Mimi could find her someone as well. Hell, she deserved it. Shit, everyone did, but some more than others.

A knock sounded on my door. I pulled back the blankets, got out of bed wearing only black boxers, and opened the heavy door.

"Mimi, you okay?" I asked, opening the door further to let her in. She entered and started pacing.

"I want to go home, back to Ballarat."

My brows dipped. "You sure?" I'd thought she'd stay until her dad passed away.

"There's no point in being here. He doesn't want me here."

"I do" came from the doorway. Wolf stood in it, already dressed for the day.

"Taro," Mimi uttered, stalling her feet. Her head dropped, gaze to the floor. "I need to go."

Wolf, ignoring me, moved into the room and got

close to his sister. "We've always known he's a vile piece of shit, but Mother loves him still."

Mimi nodded. "I know."

"Wouldn't you want to be here for her?"

Her bottom lip trembled. "I do. It just... it hurts, Taro."

Wolf tugged her into his arms. "I know, sweetheart. I hate how he has treated you. Hate it with every bone in my body."

Mimi sucked in a shuddering breath and looked up at Wolf. "For Mother, I'll stay, as long as Ruin can stay with me."

Fuck. I had hoped to go, but Mimi knew I'd stay and help her through this. She needed to know someone had her back from home, someone who also wasn't her brother.

"You've got me, honey," I told her.

She smiled sadly over at me and then wiped at her eyes. "I'll go and see if Mother needs anything."

"All right," Taro said, and we watched her walk from the room, but not before she reached out for my hand as she passed. I took it and gave her a reassuring squeeze. She breezed out the door with her head held high, but I knew it was an act.

I glanced back to Wolf and caught him quickly averting his gaze away from me. He nodded once and moved off towards the door.

"You sleep in your suits?" I blurted, and I didn't know why.

He paused. "I sleep naked, but that's not something you need to know, right?"

I swallowed. I didn't. Why did he have to fucking say it though?

"Right," I answered. He took a couple of steps. "Why're you ignorin' me?" *Shut the fuck up, man.* I didn't care that I was no longer on his radar. It was better that way.

Then why did it burn my chest every time he kept quiet?

Christ, I should have kept my mouth shut.

Wolf turned slowly and cocked his head as he studied me. I ground my teeth together when my gut tightened.

Was the tightness for disgust about the way he looked at me with heat in his eyes?

Or did my gut act up for another reason?

Nope, fuck no, it was disgust.

There was no interest there. That was fucking laughable to even allow that random thought to brush through my mind. Especially since no other guy had caught my attention in *that* way.

Then why did I keep talking to keep him here?

Why did *I* feel like a shithead for snapping at him that morning in the kitchen?

Maybe it was because I didn't want Wolf to think I hated gay people. I didn't. I had many in my life and loved them all like family.

Wolf just got under my skin in a way I didn't understand.

"You told me to fuck off, Ruin. I've fucked off."

Lifting a hand, I ran it over my hair. "Look, I'm not homophobic or anything. I have gay people in my life back home. You scared the hell outta me that morning by sneaking up."

He dragged his top teeth over his bottom lip, and I knew it was because he was trying to hide his smirk, but he failed. He took a step back my way. My heart skipped a fucking beat, and I suddenly felt like prey. It wasn't good.

"Are you saying if I warn you beforehand, I can greet you as such again?"

"What? No." I forced a laugh. Jesus, where did he get that idea from?

Wolf hummed under his breath before smiling.

"What's that smile for?" I demanded. I didn't trust it.

Wolf shrugged. I wished Mimi was back in the room or that I hadn't stopped him when he went to walk out the first time.

"Are you attending the party tonight?" Wolf asked, taking another step my way.

I cursed under my breath when I backed up a step, and his smile turned wicked. I didn't fucking retreat from anyone. Clenching my hands at my sides, I glared at the man before me. "No." I wasn't going to go to some swank party when I could look out for Mimi in our rooms since she wasn't into it either... unless she just said that yesterday for my sake. Now I didn't know.

"Do you think I'm too hard on Mimi by having her stay?" The sudden change in subject surprised me.

"Ah, no." And I didn't.

"Why?"

I rubbed at the back of my neck. "I would have done the same for my sister. If our dickhead of a dad was alive but on his deathbed, I'd try and get Nary to stay until he passed, so she had nothing to regret for the rest of her life."

His eyes softened. "Those have been my thoughts also. But if you think she needs to get out of here, to go home, let me know. I won't stop her if it's truly what she wants."

"I know you won't. But I reckon she'll need this in the end."

"I hope so and that I haven't pushed her." He glanced towards the windows and back again. "I think a night of drinking and seeing old friends could also do her well."

I should have seen that coming.

"Meanin' you want me to get her to go."

A grin grew on his lips. "It would do her well. It's for Ryo's birthday, so it will only be friends and some family."

"You sure it's a good time to have a party with the shit goin' on with your uncle?"

"I don't cower."

"I never said you did," I told him, because I honestly didn't believe he ever would.

"The party will go on. Will you make sure Mimi comes?"

Pausing, I thought about it. Maybe a night with

friends would do her good, get her to relax a little and take her mind off things once more. "I'll try."

"That's all I could ask for." He looked to his watch. "I have to go."

"Okay." I nodded.

His gaze dipped down my body. "Are you sure you want me to go?"

My gut twisted. I looked down and saw I was half hard. "It's called mornin' wood." And that was all it was. It had nothing to do with the guy in the room who looked at me like I was dessert.

Christ. It really didn't.

"You weren't before."

"I was, you just didn't notice, and why the fuck am I explainin' anythin' to you?" Turning my back on him, I adjusted myself and begged my dick to quit trying to get attention from just anyone.

Wolf chuckled low behind me. "I think he likes my attention."

"You're wrong. I'm goin' for a shower." I started for the bathroom.

"See you tonight, Ruin," he practically purred.

I flicked a hand over my shoulder. "Whatever."

More laughter followed before my bedroom door closed. I looked down at my dick. "What the fuck, man?" Of course I didn't get an answer, but I swear to Christ, my dick had a mind of its own.

Although, it'd been a while since I got laid, and I was used to pussy whenever I wanted it.

Having a woman in my bed could happen tonight,

and suddenly I was looking forward to this party... if Mimi wanted to go.

MIMI DECIDED it would be good to attend. Even though I didn't try too hard to convince her, she caved easily. With her hand in mine, she dragged me across the damn ballroom floor towards the bar on the far side. People mingled around the place. I knew none of them except for Mimi, our guards, Ryo, and Wolf. I just didn't know where the last two were.

"Vodka and tonic," Mimi ordered and glanced at me. "What are you in the mood for?"

"Beer, anything on tap," I told the waiter. I'd have one or two, but I didn't trust the people around me, so I'd stay sober enough to take on anything that came our way.

Mimi handed me the beer before we moved off to the side of the bar to make more room for others. Mimi smiled and waved at a few people but stayed by my side.

"You can go mingle," I told her.

She shook her head. "I'm fine here."

"Mimi, enjoy your night. Go talk to people you haven't seen in a long time. I'm good on my own."

She looked up at me. "Are you sure?"

"Yeah, honey." I wouldn't tell her I'd keep an eye on her, as I wanted her to relax. She needed to unwind. I didn't like the looks some people threw her way, though.

"All right, but only because I saw an old friend. I won't be gone long."

I grinned. "Sweetheart, you ain't my keeper. Don't stress about me."

Her hand reached out, and she squeezed my arm. "I won't be long."

"Stubborn," I muttered as she made her way over to a group of women around her age. Some hugged her, welcoming her back with warm smiles. A couple stood back and glowered. Fucking bitches.

Glaring at them, I took a sip of my beer and moved back further so I hit the wall behind me. The women caught my stare, said something to Mimi's group, and walked off. Good. After another chug of beer, I glanced around the place. People danced, talked, some kissed, and that was when I saw Wolf.

Holy fuck.

My pulse picked up speed.

He'd dyed his hair.

Instead of black, it was now blond with dark roots showing through.

Jesus Christ, it suited him.

My gut twisted.

I dragged my gaze away from his hair and noticed he stood with a woman in his arms as he threw his head back, laughing at something she'd said.

He shook his head as he dipped to kiss her on the cheek, then neck.

My gut tightened more.

I really had to get my stomach checked.

Snorting, I forced my gaze away and swallowed back the last of the beer before leaning closer to the bar to place the empty glass on it. When I straightened, a sultry voice said from my other side, "Hello, I don't think we've met."

A gorgeous red-haired woman stood before me in a silky black dress and heels. She lifted her hand in front of her. I wasn't in the mood, but I wasn't a total prick either. I took her hand and pressed my lips briefly to it before I dropped it. "Hey, darlin', name's Ruin."

"Elise." She smiled as her gaze ran over me, then bit her bottom lip. Usually, my dick would wake up with that type of attention. I knew she was interested, but the fucker was fast asleep.

I shifted my gaze over her shoulder, checking on Mimi. She was still talking and looked happy. It was good to see.

"How do you know Ryo?" Elise asked.

"Through Mimi," I told her, looking back to her. I wished I had another drink to put up with this small talk.

"Oh, Wolf's sister?"

"Yeah."

She shifted closer. "Are you with her?"

"No."

"Good to know."

"What's good to know?" a new voice said. A voice I

knew, one my sleeping dick perked up at. The motherfucker.

"Wolf, it's good to see you," Elise said, tilting her head back and lifting to her toes to kiss Wolf's cheek. His light hair brushed his shoulders as he looked at me. Why did I like the new colour?

My gut clenched.

Seriously, I had to see a doctor about that.

"You also, Elise. I see you've got your sights set on our guest here."

Elise giggled, while I glared at Wolf, since it was his fault for the havoc in my gut. He smirked back at me.

"I mean, who wouldn't want to?" Elise said.

I went to look at her, but Wolf's "Indeed" had my gaze shooting straight back to him. I realised from his smug smile a second too late that's what he was looking for—my attention on him.

Straightening, I glanced to see Mimi still entertained. "Fuck, I don't need this shit," I muttered to myself. Louder, I said, "I'm gettin' a drink." I walked off without another word, even when Elise called out to me.

What the fuck was going on with me?

I needed not only my body examined, but my head as well. I shouldn't care that Wolf was back to messing with me.

CHAPTER SEVEN

RUIN

$\mathcal{I}$ wandered around while keeping close to Mimi and dodging Wolf and the mountain of women who rubbed themselves on him. Not that I cared. I didn't. Hell, it was probably the hair that got the women's attention in the first place.

Honestly, I'd had enough of hanging around fake people. It was all rich people talking crap about one another. I hadn't even seen Ryo at his own party. Hoping Mimi felt the same, I made my way over to her. I weaved through the crowd even though I wanted to shove people out of the way, simply because that was the type of mood I was in. Not only was I irritated that I didn't know what the hell was going on inside me, but

I was also pissed that Wolf drew out any type of reaction.

Mimi saw me coming and smiled. It was radiant. She was enjoying herself. I couldn't drag her away all because I wasn't. I forced a grin and curled an arm around her shoulders as I caught sight of an open door, a breeze blowing the curtain inwards.

"Are you all right?" Mimi asked.

I could feel eyes on us, but I didn't give a fuck what they thought of me, and Mimi wasn't fazed I had an arm around her. "I'm all good, babe. Just wanted to let you know I'm gonna get some air over there."

"Okay, I'll be done here soon."

I shook my head and tugged her closer. "Nah, honey, take your time. I'm good."

She rolled her eyes. "Go get your air, Ruin."

I winked and walked off, but I heard behind me, "Is he yours?"

Mimi laughed. "No, we're friends. He's here from home to keep me company."

"I could have a baby or two with him," someone said, and they all laughed.

Shaking my head, I smiled despite the sour mood. At the door, I went to move the curtain out of the way to get out, but I heard voices first and froze.

"Are you sure you want to do this?" Wolf asked.

Do what?

"I have always wanted you in my mouth," Elise replied huskily.

Wanted you in my mouth?

What the fuck?

What. The. Fuck?

I grabbed the curtain and shifted it aside to peek out. Wolf leaned against the railing facing my way. His gaze focused on the woman on her knees in front of him.

His hand reached out to caress her face. "Then undo my pants if you're that keen," he taunted.

My damn gut twisted violently when I saw her hands come up.

"I would like to please you in any way I can," Elise purred.

"I'm glad to hear you say that, Elise. Release me from my pants."

I clenched my hands on the curtain and screwed up my nose, my upper lip rising.

Did I stop this or ignore it?

Why did I want to stop this?

Why did seeing it make me sick to the gut?

Her hand slipped into his pants, but her head was in the way to see anything. Not that I wanted to, but... I *did* want to stop this.

Didn't I?

No... I didn't care what Wolf was doing.

"Good girl. Open your sweet mouth for me." Wolf's words got to me. Anger sparked and burned in my chest. Before my brain caught up with my body, I pushed the curtain aside and stepped out.

"Get up," I snarled.

Elise let out a squeal when she faced me. I got an

eyeful of Wolf's cock out of his pants and was surprised he… why wasn't he hard?

"What's going on?" Elise asked, standing.

Wolf sighed and leaned his elbows back on the railing, shaking his head. What he didn't do was put away his dick.

Moving closer, I waved a hand at him but kept my gaze up. "You gonna put that away?" I asked, a little harsh.

Wolf cocked his head to the side and smirked. "No."

Glaring, I turned on Elise. "Get the fuck outta here."

"What is this?" she asked, looking between Wolf and me.

"Nothin'," I told her.

Wolf straightened and studied his nails.

"I think I'll leave," Elise said and started for the door.

"Actually," Wolf called. Elise paused. Why hadn't he put his dick away? Elise turned back to him. Her gaze dropped to his dick; so did mine. Why was it hard now? I flicked my gaze up and his eyes, full of humour, were on me. Did I do that? Why?

I took a step back. I didn't care if I'd done that.

"What?" Elise asked.

Wolf stared at her coldly. "Before you leave. Ryo," he called. Ryo appeared from a darkened corner on the balcony with a phone in his hand.

"What's this?" Elise demanded.

"Proof you were ready to have my dick in your mouth."

"You can't—"

"I can. I did. And before you run back to that boyfriend of yours, think clearly on what you will say to him, Elise."

"What do you mean?"

"Do you think your little trip to my office didn't go unnoticed?"

How can he have a conversation with his dick out?

Elise's eyes flared. "I-I—"

"Don't even try to deny it. Whatever information you found out will stay in your mind or I will send this video to him. Do you think he'll want to keep you when you were ready to suck off his enemy?"

"He won't care. He wanted me to do anything."

"Are you certain he won't care?"

Elise's lips snapped closed, and she scowled at Wolf. Yeah, her boyfriend would care.

"Ryo, escort Elise out and search her before we release her."

"Yes, Wolf." Ryo strode over and grabbed Elise by the arm. She said no more while Ryo dragged her through the doorway. I watched them go, facing away from Wolf and his dick.

Crap. I should have followed.

"Can I ask, Ruin, why you came out to stop what was happening?"

Fuck.

Sighing, I scrubbed a hand over my face and twisted to see he still stood near the railing with his goddamn dick out. It was also still hard. Shaking my head, I walked over and leaned my elbows on the railing, snarling, "Put it away."

"No."

"Why?" I barked. "And why the fuck weren't you hard for her, but as soon as I— Actually, don't answer that." I dropped my head, eyes to the ground below where people entered or left the house.

I jumped, and my skin tingled when a hand landed on my lower back. Warm breath brushed over the side of my face when Wolf said, "She didn't interest me like you do."

I clenched my teeth together. "I said don't tell me."

Laughter sounded from the doorway. I straightened and faced the door by stepping in front of Wolf. No one would fucking see him with his dick out.

A group of people stepped onto the balcony.

"Put it away," I clipped.

His soft laughter swept over me. "It's already away." His hands dropped to my waist, and I froze. One hand disappeared, and he glided a finger down the back of my neck as his body pressed into my back. My heart knocked around in my chest like it was on speed. My dick throbbed. I wanted to rip it off for doing so, as it didn't match with my brain when I *knew* I was into women. *Only* women. His lips caressed my neck lightly. "But it's good to see you get jealous." He stepped around me and greeted the people with a smile and cheerful voice.

My feet were stuck to the floor, watching him talk with his friends as if he hadn't just had his dick out, a woman nearly suck on it, and then messed with my head.

Maybe that was normal for him.

It wasn't for me.

None of this was.

What was wrong with me?

Why Wolf?

Fucking why?

He glanced back. His eyes held heat, his smile wicked.

I had to get the fuck out of there.

He grazed his top teeth over his bottom lip, watching me over the shoulder of another man.

Jesus Christ.

Fuck me.

All right... okay.... I could admit he was good-looking in his suit and white shirt, his fancy shoes, and long dyed hair, which flowed free around his shoulders. His skin needed... needed my hands on it.

Fuck.

Had I just thought that? Yeah, I did. I fucking thought of having my darker tone on his. I used to be envious of my sister's skin colouring, since it resembled Mum's, and mine was like our father's. Darker. Only now, I liked mine more because it was a distinctive contrast to Wolf's colour.

I wanted to see them together.

I fucking did, and that thought was a holy-mother-fucking-shit moment.

He was a guy.

He had a damn dick.

There were no tits to motorboat, just a flat chest.

And I stood there on my own, checking him out, my cock throbbing in my black jeans. There was no denying my dick liked what he saw. But how? He was a dude. Was my dick sick?

Broken?

Confused?

My head—on my shoulders—was about to blow. I had to get out of there.

Then why wasn't I moving?

Why couldn't I look away from the man who was smiling over the guy's shoulder at me? Why was my heart beating faster than it ever had? Even my palms were sweating.

What did I look like to Wolf? A guy freaking out on the inside but probably looking cool as a cucumber on the outside? Actually, my eyes felt wide. My lips were parted from my heavy breaths, which had my chest rising and falling rapidly. On the outside, I could have looked like a dickhead on the verge of running for the door, if my feet would move for me.

I wasn't ready for the realisation to dawn on me.

I liked playing dumb or ignoring the facts. Because the facts showed me I was into Wolf.

A guy.

How could I switch just like that?

It was *his* fault.

His damn looks were the problem.

His teasing was the issue.

His attention on me was the trouble that caused my dick to react in the first place.

Glaring over at him, I remained frozen, which caused him to laugh. The man he spoke to went to turn to look at what had him amused, but Wolf brought his attention back by taking his arm.

The fucking prick touched a guy in front of me.

"Ruin?"

I swung my gaze down to Mimi. When had she got out there? She glanced from me to her brother and back again.

"Hey, you done?" I asked.

"Sure. Everything okay?"

"Yep." I nodded and wouldn't allow my gaze to shoot back to Wolf like it wanted to. Instead, I curled an arm around her shoulders and guided her towards the door.

Mimi's hand lifted and gripped my waist. "You sure everything's okay?"

"Course." I smiled down at her.

"Are you going?"

I stilled at the words, knowing who they'd come from. Mimi looked up at me and then to her brother, since I wouldn't. "Yes. It's been great catching up with people, but I'm all done socialising."

"I understand. I wish I could leave also." Wolf reached out to take Mimi's hand, and he pulled her into a hug. I glanced up, and our gazes locked. Wolf smiled, my gut twisted, and I glared in return. His smile increased, and he winked. I looked away.

When Mimi wound her arm around my waist again, I took it as a sign to continue to the door.

"Goodnight, Ruin" was called from behind me.

"Yeah, night," I replied shortly.

Botan and Mimi's guard stayed back as we walked down the hall, and Mimi filled me in on some of her friends. At her door, she unlocked it and pushed it open but didn't enter.

"You know," she started, and I pulled my eyes from glancing down the hall to her, "it's okay."

I dipped my brows, confused. "What is?"

"If you like my brother."

I scoffed, snorted, and forced an awkward laugh. "You've had too much to drink," I told her, shaking my head. Fear upped my pulse. Had she sensed something between us? How? I…. Wasn't Wolf like that with everyone?

Mimi gave me a soft smile. Her hand rested on my arm as I crossed them over my chest. "Ruin, I know we're friends, and no offense, but I wouldn't want to date you because you're like a brother now. I won't be hurt if anything happened between you and Taro."

Even though my gut clenched and my heart raced, I rolled my eyes. Shit, I hadn't even thought that— jumping from one sibling to another—and I wouldn't need to because nothing was going on with me and Taro—Wolf. Fucking *Wolf*. "Are you forgetting I'm into women?" Christ, those words tasted disgusting. *Why?*

Ignore.

Ignore.

Ignore.

Mimi sighed. "People can change."

"Not this one."

"Your parents would support you," she tried.

"They don't need to. There's nothing to support."

Mimi groaned as if in pain. "Ruin. I'm not blind. I see some... chemistry between you and Taro." So what if she had? But I still didn't get how. I hadn't done anything... had I?

I shook my head. "You must be going blind."

Her lips thinned. "You're annoying me now."

I shrugged and smirked. "Okay."

"I want to kick you."

Chuckling, I said, "No need to get violent."

Her other hand also gripped my arm as she stepped closer. "It would be scary knowing you have this new feeling inside you—"

"Mimi," I warned. What was she, psychic?

"But life is about challenges and acceptance. Live your life, Ruin, in any way you want it. I took a chance and ran when I had to, and it was the best choice I made because it brought me to a new family. A daunting one to begin with, but one that holds so much love no matter who you are. Taro's a good guy. Take your chance... when you're ready."

Glaring, I looked away from her. "I don't know why you're telling me all this shit for."

Mimi hummed under her breath. "You stubborn, pain-in-the-arse dick."

I was. I really was.

Snorting, I asked, "You comin' on to me, babe?"

It was her turn to glare as she shook her head and stepped back. "I wish my brother luck with you."

I was the one who needed luck when it came to her brother, but I didn't say that. Instead, I said, "Night, sweetheart."

"Night, pest," she said, smiling as she closed the door.

I didn't like that Mimi could read something between Wolf and me. Not when I... wasn't ready to accept anything, because the fucking thought of change scared me. I liked my life as it was. I liked who I was, and now, it was as if I didn't know myself.

CHAPTER EIGHT

WOLF

*T*he other night, Ruin's dismissal at Ryo's birthday when we'd stood with Elise at the bar annoyed me. He always ran whenever I got close. He hadn't even complimented my change in hair colour.

There was something about Ruin that appealed to me. It was beside the fact he was stunningly gorgeous. I had never been attracted to the tattooed hooligan type, who didn't like the letter *G* on the end of words or wouldn't wear a suit if his life depended on it.

As soon as I had seen him back in Ballarat standing off to the side from his biker brothers, listening, waiting, it had been hard to concentrate on the matter, and all because he had taken my breath away. His beauty was like no other.

I'd wanted to know him, taste him, and use his name by ruining him in the best way.

Luck had been on my side when the club's president ordered Ruin to watch over Mimi. I had been offended at first—that Talon would think I would do anything to my sister. I was nothing like my father. But I caved quickly when I knew I wanted more time gazing at the wonder before me.

I sounded like a perverted stalker, but it was what Ruin did to me. I couldn't stop myself from teasing him, hoping to get a rise, and when I did, his eyes came to life.

I was sure I saw something in them each time, as if he enjoyed my attention. Except for that unfortunate slip-up in the kitchen when I couldn't resist any longer and had to have my hands and lips on him.

His look of disgust still angered me, but the confusion I also saw puzzled me.

I wanted to piece the puzzle together and see what the picture revealed when our time together finished.

He would leave to go home, and I would be stuck here in charge of the family.

I couldn't help but think of that night once more. The way he had stormed onto the balcony to stop Elise, much like a scorned lover. When I saw him like that, I had hardened over it and was glad he took notice. I wanted to take him into my arms, have his mouth on mine while I ground my hardness into him.

I definitely was a man with a crush.

Could I win him over?

I didn't know. Even when I thought I saw interest, I wasn't sure he would dive into something with me. His grumpiness covered his shyness when it came to our interaction. Did I risk pushing him when all we could have was the time we had together now?

"Ryo, plans for the day?" I asked as we made our way towards the kitchen, having missed breakfast. My friend wasn't only the head of security and my personal bodyguard, but he had taken on the role of my assistant as well. To be honest, I would be lost without him.

"Besides the mountain of paperwork and requests from family members?"

"Yes, besides that."

"Your uncle's meeting is at 2:00 p.m. The Ito family head has called again and wishes to meet with you. Sensei has moved your training to 6:00 p.m."

Another full day. Another day I wouldn't see Ruin, and already it had been a few since the party. It surprised me how much I missed seeing him, teasing him.

"Any updates on Father?"

"His heart has weakened even more. They're saying any day now."

If he was any other man but the cold, cruel one I had been brought up by, I would have felt something when I heard those words, but I didn't. Maybe I would when he did pass, but I doubted it. Although, any pain would be for my mother and her losing the one she loved.

Voices drew my attention down the hall. Botan and Nobu stood outside the kitchen, so I knew who was inside, and my heart fluttered. Ruin. I liked the thought of seeing him so much, I smiled. However, after nodding to the guards, I paused and listened to their conversation.

"I don't know, Ruin."

"Come on, Mimi. You'll have fun, and it'll take your mind off things."

"But I don't know anyone in the Caroline Springs charter."

"You'll love them as much as you do the Ballarat charter. I promise."

I heard Mimi sigh. "Fine. But you have to stick to my side."

"Like glue. So, I can text them back and tell them we'll be there?"

"Yes. God, you're like an excited little puppy."

Ruin laughed. "I've been here nearly three weeks and haven't seen the brothers yet. Course I'm excited."

Stepping around the door, I asked, "Where are we going?"

Mimi smiled, while Ruin froze, gazing down at his phone in the middle of a text. A slight blush touched his cheeks, and I wanted to brush my fingers over it.

"Ruin's taking me to the Hawks bar tonight," Mimi explained.

"Am I invited?" I queried.

Ryo made a noise in the back of his throat. I glanced there to see his eyes were on Ruin's. I looked back to the biker and found his chest rising and falling quickly. His eyes wider than usual.

"I… I'm not sure. I can't invite you. Ruin?" Mimi said, a small smile playing on her lips. Was my sister helping me unconsciously, or did she suspect something and this was her approval? I hoped for the second, as I worried if anything did happen, Mimi would be upset. If that had been the case, I wouldn't try for anything.

Ruin finished the text, pocketed the phone, and looked up. "Not sure it'd be your kinda place."

Did he not know that any place he would be was the right place?

"I'm sure it will be fine."

He swung his gaze to Mimi, seeking help, but she just smiled. His eyes narrowed. "Yeah, all right, if you want to. Ryo, you can come also, but we ain't taking the guards. I'll have Mimi's back, as will my brothers."

"Thank you for the invite," Ryo answered.

Ruin grunted.

"What time are we leaving?"

"I'm takin' my ride, and at six."

"I'll be ready. Ryo—"

"Already cancelling, Wolf."

"Excellent." Moving over to the coffee maker, which happened to be by Ruin, I asked, "Would anyone like a coffee?"

"I will make it," Ryo offered. When I glared, he turned his back, but I saw his shoulders shaking.

"I'm good, thanks," Mimi said.

When I stopped at Ruin's side, he seemed tenser than before. "Ruin?" I said softly.

"Sure," he replied.

"Milk and one sugar?"

His attention snapped to me. "How'd you know?"

I had overheard the cooks mentioning his coffee preference. I shrugged. "A guess." I reached around him to grab the sugar canister and took in a deep breath. He always smelled delicious. I bit my bottom lip and met his gaze. When he swallowed thickly, I smiled and finished making the coffees.

In the background, Mimi spoke to Ryo, but I was too focused on the man next to me. Ruin shifted, and I was sure he adjusted himself in his jeans, but when I looked, he was leaning back against the counter.

"For you," I said, handing him his coffee.

His hand shook a little when he reached for it, until he clenched his teeth and glared down at the mug as if it offended him. "Thanks," he mumbled.

Turning with my mug in hand, I asked, "Are you sure you won't mind me coming?"

He choked and spat coffee out. Puzzled, I cocked my head to the side and thought over my words, then started laughing.

"You have a dirty mind, Ruin," I commented.

His face was red as he pounded his chest.

"Are you all right?" Mimi asked.

Ruin nodded. For the first time, I wondered what his real name was. I doubted his parents had named him Ruin.

"Fine," Ruin coughed out. He glared out the corner of his eye at me. "And I wasn't thinking *that*."

"Really? Then what were you thinking?" I teased.

"Nothing, I just took it down the wrong way." I snorted. He groaned and quickly added, "The coffee."

"Sure," I drew out and glanced over to see Mimi and Ryo watching us. Both had smiles on their faces.

Ruin must have also noticed, because he quickly straightened and announced, "Gonna hit the gym. You up for it, Mimi?"

"Sure," Mimi said, climbing off her stool.

"See you both tonight," I said.

Ruin nodded. "Yeah."

It would be a sight watching Ruin work out, but I'd already had my fill of him, and I didn't want to fluster him more than necessary, or else he would revoke his offer for me to go to the bar. Something I was looking forward to. Though, if I was honest, I was a little nervous walking into a bar run by bikers who hardly knew me, but they probably knew of my family name and businesses. Still, I wouldn't miss seeing Ruin in his own element. It could show me more about the man than I already knew.

Once they were gone, after a quick hug from Mimi, Ryo turned to me. "Are you certain you want to walk into a Hawks bar?"

"No doubt they would have more information on me and the family's dealings by now."

"No doubt, and from what I have learned, they're a clean club. Refuse to deal in anything illegal. I have heard the only trouble they get into is when it involves someone they care about."

"Then I guess we'll see how they react to me going."

"Wolf, our family runs drugs and weapons."

"You're not surprising me in this. I do know."

"I know you know, but their club is large and all over Australia. We do not want any trouble with them."

"Talon already knows we don't want trouble, else I wouldn't have given up my own men when they went out on their own and messed with their club."

Ryo sighed. "I thought the Hawks would only be in our lives for a short time, but I see how wrong I was."

"They took care of Mimi, and she wants to return there once this is done here. As long as she has them in her life, then I will also."

"Will they accept you though?"

"Only time will tell. I'll have a meeting with Talon once she goes back and make sure he understands what it will entail, having a Takahashi family member in their lives."

"That it comes with putting up with random visits from the head of house?"

"Yes. I will not lose my sister again."

"And this has nothing to do with a certain biker? That he'll be back there with her?"

Glancing away, I said, "Not at all."

"With respect, Taro-sama, but you are full of shit."

Snorting, I commented, "You're lucky we have been lifelong friends, Ryo."

"I know this. Let's eat and get some work done."

Yes, because the sooner the day sped by, the better. It would mean more time around Ruin.

CHAPTER NINE

WOLF

*T*he drive took over an hour to get to the bar, but I didn't care since it gave me time to speak with Mimi. When I asked why she didn't go with Ruin, she informed me she wasn't allowed on the back of Ruin's bike because she wasn't his "old lady." Mimi went on to explain they were what the bikers called their girlfriends or intended wives.

"Taro," Mimi said. I didn't want to look away from Ruin on his ride. He wore a long-sleeve Henley, a club vest, and leather pants.

Leather pants.

The view was nicely seared into my mind because they hugged his arse sweetly.

"Hmm?" I answered as Ryo turned the car into a street, following Ruin.

"You like Ruin, don't you?"

Turning in my seat, I told her, "He... appeals to me."

Ryo snorted. I ignored him.

"I just wanted you to know it's okay with me if you do. But Ruin has become a friend. You need to be careful with him."

"Careful in what way?"

"He's never been into guys."

"I know."

"He's fighting this."

My heart expanded in my chest. "Are you saying you see something from him towards me?"

I had thought I'd seen signs, but having reassurance from another party wouldn't hurt. I didn't want to push further if I was wrong and the "interest" was all in my head.

"I'm pretty sure I am."

I could not contain my smile as I faced forward and caught Ruin pulling into a parking area in front of a crowded bar. "Then I'll be careful with him."

Mimi's hand rested on my shoulder. "Good luck."

"Thank you, and Mimi?"

"Yes?"

"It's good to have you here." In Melbourne, back with me.

"Love you," she whispered before climbing out of the car as Ryo parked.

"Are you ready?" Ryo asked.

I watched Mimi approach Ruin as he climbed off his bike and removed his helmet. His smile was broad, happy. I liked seeing it.

I wasn't ready and could not believe my nerves had risen once more over walking into a bar the Hawks owned. Usually, I didn't care where I went or what people thought, but this time it mattered to me... because of him.

"Yes," I said, and got out of the car. When I closed my door, a little too roughly, Ruin's gaze lifted my way. I caught him quickly scan over my body. A small smirk played on his lips, and a slight shake of his head followed.

I might have gone a little overboard wearing a suit, with my long white jacket over it. Ruin's reaction was worth it, however. He had been getting his bike out of the garage when I got into the car, his bug-eyed double take doing wonders for my ego.

Ryo met me at the front of the car, and we walked to Ruin and Mimi. "You guys aren't armed, right?"

I winced. "Well...."

Ruin groaned. "Please put them in the damn car. Nothin' will happen to anyone since you're walkin' in with me."

"Wolf is protected at all times, no matter where we are or with who," Ryo said curtly.

I placed my hand on Ryo's arm. He looked at me. "I'm sure it will be fine, for tonight."

"I don't—"

"Ryo," I warned.

Ryo shot his gaze to Ruin and glared, only Ruin didn't see it. Instead, his gaze was down on my hand on Ryo's arm. Interesting. When I removed it, he seemed to blink out of his daze and said, "You got my word we'll keep him safe."

"Fine," Ryo snapped as he turned and started for the car.

"Ryo," I called and took the gun from my holster at my hip, holding it out. Ryo stomped back for it, grumbling under his breath. When he had it in hand, he knew to wait while I removed the gun on my right ankle, the dagger on my left, and the others on each wrist.

"Fucking hell," Ruin muttered while Mimi giggled.

We waited in silence while Ryo secured our weapons. As soon as he was back, Ruin started for the door with Mimi at his side. I didn't mind being behind him at all, as I got to see him move in those pants.

When he opened the door, the music hit us, yet it wasn't loud enough to drive someone crazy if all they wanted to do was talk. Stepping in, the atmosphere was calm, the place set out neatly. Ruin moved over towards the right side of the bar, where many other bikers stood with some women.

"Ruin" was yelled. Many approached, back slaps the standard greeting between the men. I didn't miss the uncertain and sometimes hostile gazes Ryo and I got. Thankfully, Mimi was spared from them, especially when she was the first introduced.

"And this is her brother, Wolf, and their friend Ryo,"

Ruin explained. I wouldn't have exactly downplayed it that way, but maybe he thought it would be safer.

"Aren't you the boss of the Takahashi family?" a man with a baseball cap on questioned.

I nodded. "Yes."

Another man, this one bigger than the others, moved his hands in clear sign language. Ruin replied in the same way and said aloud, "They're here to have a good night."

Ruin knew sign language. I didn't let on that I also did, but it was good to know.

The big man grunted.

"There'll be no trouble from us," I told them. The men still looked wary, and I couldn't say I blamed them.

"Mimi, Wolf, Ryo, this here is Pick"—he wore the baseball cap—"Billy"—he was blond—"Beast"—the big man who signed—"Knife"—a man with darker hair— "Dive"—large man with steel eyes—"and Handle"—who had facial hair and tattoos. Actually, a lot of them did. "I'll introduce you to the others hangin' around soon."

"Precious," Pick called. "Get your sweet arse over here."

A stunning red-haired woman who had been talking to a blonde rolled her eyes, said one last thing, and then made her way over. What surprised me was that Billy curled her into his side, yet Pick smiled down at her like she was his world.

Pick took her hand and used his other to gesture to my sister. "Baby, this is Mimi. Mimi, our woman, Josie."

Our woman?

Our woman?

Ryo and I glanced at each other with our brows raised.

"Hey, Mimi." Josie smiled.

"Hi, nice to meet you. I'm... um, living at the compound in Ballarat, so I've heard about you from Zara, your sister."

Josie smiled. "How is she?"

"Good, the last time I saw her. I, ah, don't mingle too much."

Josie smiled softly. "I can understand that. Do you want to come meet some of the other old ladies?"

Mimi glanced at us and then back. "Sure?"

"Mimi," Ruin called. "You're cool to stay here if you want to. Or you can come to the table over there with me." He nodded to a table Knife and Beast had gone to.

"It's okay. I'll come over there soon."

"Ryo" was all I said.

"I'll get drinks," he replied.

"Can my brother come with us?" Mimi quickly asked while Ryo walked off to the bar.

Josie glanced up at Pick, who looked to Ruin, and he gave a small nod. If I understood correctly, Pick was checking if I could be trusted around their women, and Ruin just told him I could be. I couldn't decline the offer now, even when I wanted to sit with Ruin and hear things about him.

"Of course," Josie said. "Coming?" she asked me.

If I said no, I guessed I would be frowned on by the bikers for ignoring their women. "I would like to." I took Mimi's hand in mine, and we followed Josie over to another table full of women. Even though I preferred men as lovers, I didn't mind the company of women. It could come to my advantage of getting information on Ruin also.

"Who we got here, Josie-girl?" a woman with wild dark hair asked. Before Josie could say anything, she went on with "Ruin, get your cute butt here and give Low some sugar."

A deep chuckle sounded behind me. Ruin moved around and hugged the woman named Low. "Where's Dodge at?"

"In the back room giving Rommy another lecture."

"What happened?"

"Tell you about it later." She grinned. "Go greet the others while Josie introduces us to your people."

His people. I liked hearing that.

"Bossy as ever," Ruin teased.

She laughed and patted his cheek. "Of course."

I watched as Ruin moved his way around and greeted every woman like they were his family. It made sense, since I heard the members of the club classed everyone as family.

Josie cleared her throat, and I looked back to see Low studying me when Josie said, "This is Mimi. She lives at the compound in Ballarat and is friends with Ruin, and this is her brother, Wolf. The gentleman at the bar is Ryo." She glanced at me. "I hope I have that right."

"You do," I told her with a smile.

Low whistled. "Damn, boy, that hair, that body, and you have some sweet cheekbone structure going on. You must be popular with the ladies?"

My smile widened. "I cannot complain." I had a feeling she was fishing to see if I preferred men.

"I bet," she mumbled. "Come take a seat."

A squeal echoed around the room. "Ruin!" A woman ran by us and launched herself at Ruin, who caught her easily. Distaste thickened my throat as I pulled up my top lip in a silent snarl. I didn't like how he held her close. How he placed her on her feet and cupped her cheeks, beaming down at her.

"Fascinating," I heard and looked back to see Low once again studying me. Mimi had already sat beside Josie while I stood there like an idiot staring at Ruin.

I didn't comment back. Instead, I took the seat next to her and leaned back in the chair, acting calm when all I wanted to do was drag Ruin away from that woman. It would have been best to have picked a different seat. From this position, I had a good view of the people in the bar, including of the sweet look Ruin was giving the woman.

"Wolf," Ryo said before placing a gin and tonic on the table.

"Thank you," I replied, and quickly took up the drink for a long gulp while he went to Mimi to hand hers over.

Why did I want to come?

I sighed internally since I wanted to know more about Ruin and see him around his people.

"That's Rommy," Low said, and I lifted my gaze from the glass to see she was looking at me.

"Sorry?" I asked just when Ryo took the seat next to me.

Low pointed from Ryo and me, bluntly asking, "You two together?"

Ryo choked on his sip, shaking his head.

"No," I replied. "Ryo is my assistant."

Low's brows rose. "An assistant who works this late and comes to bars with you?"

"Low, stop interrogating them," Josie said.

"I think it's fun," Mimi commented.

I glared over at her. "Ryo is also my personal guard."

"You must be important," a blonde woman asked. "Sorry, my name's Mena. I'm with Dive, and this is Della. She's with Handle."

"Nice to meet you all. I'm Wolf, and this is Mimi and Ryo. To answer your question, I run the Takahashi family. We have a lot of businesses."

"Must have some enemies to have a guard with you," Low said.

I smirked. "Some."

She hummed under her breath and pointed over to the men. I glanced there to see Ruin at the table with the other bikers, his arm around the woman. Another man stood with them. "As I was saying, that's Rommy with Ruin. She's mine and Dodge's girl. Good friends with Ruin."

Friends. Were they only friends?

I went to turn my attention back to Low, but something else caught my eye. The man named Beast had his hand gripping the back of Knife's neck in a claiming manner. Knife turned to look up at Beast with a warm smile. He said something that had Beast's eyes heating.

Low knocked my arm. "Yeah, they're together, but it's best not to stare too long because one or both of them will rip your head off if they think you're into one of them."

"Together?"

"That's what I said."

I leaned closer to Low and asked, "Pick introduced Josie as his and Billy's."

Low laughed. "Lucky bitch has got the both of them twisted around her finger. They're all totally devoted to one another."

A new feeling expanded in my chest. I didn't quite understand it, but it was part jealousy and envy, if I had to guess. They could all love who they wanted and didn't care what anyone thought. I was only becoming that way after many years. This was what I wanted for my family, but I doubted I could ever have a connection of trust and acceptance within the family like these people had.

Mena started speaking with Ryo, and Mimi was still distracted by Josie and Della when Low leaned closer. "You're into our boy Ruin, hey?"

Was it that obvious?

I didn't say anything in case it would upset Ruin in some way. Low snorted. "It's cool. You don't have to say anything. I can tell." She put her elbow to the table and rested her chin on that hand, looking at me. "Just know that if you hurt him, there will be many coming after you."

I clenched my jaw. "You have nothing to fear from me. Ruin isn't into men." I was an idiot. I fell right into her trap and gave my feelings away anyway.

She hummed under her breath. She picked up her glass and held it out to me. "Cheers to the future."

This woman puzzled me, especially that glint in her eyes. I clinked my glass against hers and answered, "Yes, cheers."

I was happy for Ruin and what he had with these people. His family. They cared, and it was certain they would continue loving him no matter who he ended up with.

Did I dare hope it would be me?

Not yet.

CHAPTER TEN

RUIN

*W*e'd been there about an hour. Mimi looked like she was having fun with the women since she hadn't come to seek me out, staying with them the whole time—even when others had switched tables and mingled.

I hadn't moved from the brothers' table, though, because Wolf was still sitting over with Low, and now Dodge, speaking with them.

Every time I saw him since that night on the balcony, I got flustered, having dreamt about him ever since. He had really gotten into my head, and I didn't know what to do about that. I didn't know how to act, besides being a fool whenever I saw him in the house, where I quickly ducked into another room to avoid him.

Once, and with the worst possible timing, Katon saw me just after I'd army rolled into a room he was exiting. I'd knocked the poor guy over. Fortunately, I'd caught him before he'd done any damage, but hearing Wolf and Ryo approaching, I'd panicked and covered Katon's mouth.

I'd apologised for my actions, and thankfully, from his smile, he'd thought it was funny, but I felt like the biggest idiot. Quickly, I'd realised I had to stop dodging Wolf and deal with whatever this was between us. It had been the next morning that Wolf caught Mimi and me in the kitchen and invited himself to the pub.

"Another round?" Dive asked as he stood.

"I'm good, brother. Gonna ride back."

"I'll take one," Knife said, and Beast signed he wasn't going to have one since he'd be driving. Dive tipped his chin up and went off to the bar where Fang was serving. Billy pulled out a chair beside me, flipped it backwards, and sat down.

"You know," he started, "that Wolf guy can't keep his eyes off you."

My face burned. I had a feeling of being watched but hearing it from someone else confirmed it. There was also the fact that every time I glanced over there, Wolf was already looking my way.

"You're seein' things," I told him stupidly.

Knife snorted. "Brother, I've noticed it as well."

I shrugged. "Then you're both crazy."

Beast rose a brow at me. *"Not crazy,"* he signed.

"He a problem for you?" Billy asked.

"No," I muttered. Even though he was because I couldn't stop thinking about him.

"You know it's cool if you like dick," Knife said.

I choked on my own saliva. "What the fuck, man?"

His hands went out. "What?" He smirked.

"Fuck off." I glared.

"Ruin," Billy said. "You won't have a problem with any brother if you're thinkin' about somethin' with him. We know his background. We know he runs drugs and guns. As long as none of it brushes off on Hawks, you can take a chance."

Crossing my arms over my chest, I clipped, "Nothin' to take a chance on."

"I used to be like that," Knife said.

"What?" I stupidly asked.

"In denial. But, brother, the gazing hasn't been just comin' from him. Don't deny yourself when, in the end, it could work out for the better. Know it did for me."

Beast leaned in and kissed the back of Knife's neck, causing Knife to grin at the big guy.

I was swimming in so much denial I could choke on it, but the thought of dragging myself out of it and doing something about my attraction, or whatever the fuck it was, scared the fuck out of me more than anything.

"Word of warnin' though," Knife said. "Don't try wax."

Laughter burst out of me. "What?"

Knife shuddered while Beast chuckled. Knife shook his head. "Nothin', just trust me."

"Wax hasn't even crossed my mind."

He pointed at me. "Good, leave it that way."

"Hey, hey, hey," Rommy called, skipping up to us. She curled her arms around my shoulders and rested her chin on them. "Who's going to dance with me?"

"Not me, darlin'," Knife said. Beast shook his head.

"I've gotta take over the bar shift soon," Billy said.

"Ruin?" she pleaded.

"Uh-oh, someone doesn't like seein' the attention Ruin's gettin'," Knife said.

"Huh?" Rommy asked.

Knife shook his head, smirking. "Nothin', sweetheart."

"Can I sit here?"

My heart skipped a beat and raced off along with my pulse when I looked up to Wolf standing beside the table.

"Do *you* want to dance?" Rommy asked Wolf.

Wolf smiled, my gut twisted, and it was time to admit my gut acted in that way because of the attraction I felt.

I liked the look of Wolf. His smile, looks, mannerism, words.

Fuck me.

"Thank you for the offer, but not tonight."

"Dang it," Rommy said with a pout.

"Rommy, why don't you try the women?" Knife asked.

She sighed. "All right, but every time they get on the dance floor, the men drag their women off because of the guys watching them."

I snorted while the others laughed. Billy stood. "Can't be helped, Rom, but I'm sure the ladies will dance with you even if it's for a short time."

She smiled. "You're right." She kissed my cheek and quickly disappeared.

"Here, take my seat," Billy offered to Wolf before he moved off to the bar. Of course, it was right next to mine. There were others at the table, but he did as Billy said, only turned it back around before sitting. Close.

"Am I interrupting something?" Wolf asked.

"Nah, we're just shootin' the shit," Knife answered. He leaned back in his chair and eyed the man next to me.

I could feel Wolf's gaze on me. It burned in a funny, tingly way. "So, Joshua," Wolf uttered, and I stilled.

The women had been talking.

"Taro," I countered.

Beast knocked the table, and I looked there. His smirk was teasing. *"He looks at you like he wants to eat you."*

Wolf chuckled. We all stared in shock when his hands moved around. *"This is true."*

Knife cracked up, Beast chuckled, but I about pissed myself.

Wolf knew sign language. How?

"How do you know sign language?" Beast asked. I was grateful, as I couldn't seem to move.

This is true. He'd said that to my brothers. That he wanted to eat me. Wasn't I supposed to be grossed out by knowing that?

I wasn't.

In fact, my body reacted the opposite to the information.

Heart, pulse, gut. All of them went haywire and.... Christ, I wanted to reach over and take his mouth.

I wanted to kiss a man.

They spoke back and forth about stuff I didn't take note of, and I watched Wolf easily charm my brothers as they laughed about something.

If I wasn't sitting in a bar, would I have the guts to do something about this attraction? Would I have the nerve to actually kiss him?

There went my stomach twisting in that same way from the thought of taking his mouth.

"Ruin?"

Goddamn, I wished I was any place but here so I could test myself and see if I'd do anything.

"Ruin?"

Why did it have to be him?

What made him different from any other guy? Shit, I'd known good-looking guys throughout my life. I had other guys hit on me, and none of them stirred something up inside of me like this.

"Joshua?" Wolf uttered, and I blinked from a daze.

"Huh?" I glanced to Knife and Beast. The first was smirking while taking a sip of his new beer. When had Dive brought it back? The second was chuckling low.

A hand touched my arm, and I looked down at it.

He had such pale skin. So different to mine.

"Are you all right?" Wolf asked.

Knife snorted and commented, "I'm guessin' he is, but busy sortin' his head out."

I nodded. "I'm good." I couldn't meet his gaze, though, aware my face was hot from being lost in my own thoughts of the man next to me. "You think Mimi is ready to go?"

"I'll go see," Wolf said and stood, making his way to the dance floor where Mimi was with Rommy.

"Babe, give us a moment," Knife said. Beast stood and reached over to grip my shoulder. He lifted his chin at me, and I returned it.

"What?" I asked Knife when Beast walked over to the bar where Billy was.

"Like I said, it's scary shit to start with, but if you got this cravin', it's best to give it a go so you don't regret anythin' in the end."

"Knife," I groaned, running a hand over my face.

Knife clasped my shoulder. "Brother, listen to me. Things change in life for a reason, and maybe your reason is on that dance floor tryin' to get his sister to leave because he knows you want to go. I fought what I felt for Beast because women were my thing before Beast opened me up to somethin' else. Don't kill yourself over this. There ain't anythin' wrong with likin' a guy."

"I know that."

"Good. Because I reckon it only happens to the best of us."

"What?"

"Seein' that there's more to life than what we originally thought. Takin' a chance on somethin' new that could lead into somethin' good."

I clenched my jaw. "His family is fucked up."

"He might need the support."

"I don't even know...."

"What?"

"If I could.... Jesus." I shook my head.

"If you could do anythin' with a guy?"

I shrugged. "Maybe."

"You won't unless you try. But not tryin' is givin' up. It's up to you which way you wanna go about it."

"You... liked it?"

Knife chuckled. "Like? Brother, no. I fuckin' love it, because it's with the right person. If it was anyone else but that big lug, I wouldn't have done shit about it."

Beast was Knife's one.

That was why he went for it.

But would Taro be my one?

I couldn't see it yet, but did I give up on the chance to figure it out?

Could I ignore this attraction?

No.

No, I couldn't, because Knife was right. I would regret it in the end.

Now I just had to find the balls to do something about it.

CHAPTER ELEVEN

RUIN

We'd been back for about twenty minutes. Everyone had headed to their own rooms, but along the way, Mimi kept saying how much fun she'd had. She loved my brothers and sisters, and I was glad for it. I could tell they enjoyed her company just as much.

Taro had been quiet though.

Taro... when had I started to think of him by his real name?

I liked using Wolf, but there was something about using his real name that was... special.

Groaning, I cupped my head in my hands as I sat on the edge of my bed. I couldn't sleep. All I could do was think about him.

I wanted to charge to his room and demand answers on how he'd bewitched me. I wanted an argument. I wanted a fight. I wanted... to go and kiss him to see if my head, dick, and gut had just been acting up and whatever I felt was only in my imagination.

Would now be a good time to test it out?

Standing, I fisted my hands and stomped to the bedroom door, only to pause with my hand on the door handle.

Dropping my hand, I looked down at myself, still dressed in what I wore to the bar, minus my shoes and socks. This was all right to wear when going to the bedroom of a guy who you may or may not kiss. Right?

I didn't want to rock up naked. Taro could get the wrong idea, and I wasn't ready for the next move just yet.

Fuck me, when did I turn into such a pussy? If a woman didn't approach me, I'd be the one to seek them out and get what I want. Mainly an orgasm. I didn't second-guess myself, look at my clothes or worry about... shit, my breath. I quickly went into the bathroom and brushed my teeth.

I was going to do this.

I was.

And without another thought, I stormed to my bedroom door, swung it open, and took the few steps to stop in front of Taro's door.

I didn't pause. I didn't piss myself. I didn't chicken out.

I lifted my hand and knocked once.

If he didn't answer, I would go back to my room and—

The door swung open. Taro stood in the doorway wearing a pair of silk sleep pants. His body, Christ... smooth, beautiful pale skin.

He reached out, wrapped a hand in my Henley, and dragged me into the room. The door slammed closed. I was pushed up against the wall before his body pressed against me and his mouth was on mine.

His. Mouth. Was. On. *Mine.*

Fuck.

Lust exploded. I cupped his cheeks and deepened the kiss with a groan. Our tongues tangled, fought, and demanded from one another. I slid a hand to the back of his head and tugged, gaining control of the kiss, and when he moaned, I drank it down.

Taro pushed his hardness against me, and when he paused for a moment, I knew he felt I was just as hard. In fact, my dick throbbed.

I glided my hand from his cheek down over his flat chest, gently rubbing across his nipple, which brought out a shudder from him. I grunted into the kiss, liking the thought of him reacting to me.

His hands on my waist tightened. They slid up to the back of my neck and held on as he allowed me to take my fill of touching him.

My hands shifted over his body like they were made to. Down his waist, hips, lower back, and finally his arse, where I held each rounded, perky cheek tightly in my hands, forcing his cock to rub against mine.

This…. Never had I been taken over like this, lost to just touch and taste.

His hands moved to my shoulders when I kissed down his neck. He arched for me. Both of us held heavy breaths, but I wanted more. I wanted to taste him everywhere. Touch every inch of him.

Him.

Taro.

A guy.

Panic surfaced, making my gut drop.

Resting my forehead to his shoulder, I sucked in a deep breath. My grip on him loosened. He rubbed up and down my arms.

"It's okay. It's all right," he said.

I shook my head. It wasn't.

I didn't understand this. I couldn't work out why I'd changed because of him… but I knew I didn't want to miss out on this connection.

Not when it was already something big from even just one kiss.

Because I fucking wanted more.

I shook my head, lifted it enough to press my lips against his throat, and drew in his scent. Taro let out a shaky breath, which hitched when I gripped his arse.

"What have you done to me?" I whispered.

"I-I think it's the other way around. What you've done to me."

I nipped at his skin, and his fingers dug into my arms.

"Josh," he uttered.

"Say it again," I ordered.

"Josh," he whispered, his breath hitching once more when I sucked on his neck, marking him.

Fuck.

Christ.

I wanted to mark him all over.

Where the hell was this coming from?

What *had* he done to me?

Pulling my mouth from him, I tugged his head back using his hair and stared into his glazed eyes. I ran mine over his porcelain skin, his sharp cheekbones, his gorgeous dark eyes, his nose, chin, lips.

The fear vanished as I stared at the man who'd consumed me for the last few weeks.

"You like me," I told him.

"Yes," he said softly.

"Okay." I nodded.

"Josh—"

Cutting him off, I kissed him, clutching him to me, holding on to him like my life depended on it. Taro returned the fierce need and rubbed himself against me.

I wanted him.

I wanted all of him.

But not yet.

For once in my life, I didn't want to just fuck a

person and get them out of my system before moving to the next.

I wanted to savour every second we had together and not rush into anything sexual.

Breaking the kiss, I rested my forehead against his. "Who told you my name?"

"Huh?" He blinked and eased his head back to look at me.

Sliding my palms to his waist, I then took his hand and pulled him over to the bed. He seemed a little stunned by my actions, which was good as I twisted us and dropped to the bed. I pulled him up and over me. I would have left him on top of me, but that position would lead to something more, so I moved him to the side, where he lay half on and off the bed with me on his side.

"What are you doing?" he asked, his eyes a little wide.

"Talkin'," I said with a smirk. I shifted us again and rolled to my side to face him. I reached out and traced his bottom lip with a finger. "Who told you my real name?"

"Does it matter?" he asked breathily.

"Not really."

His eyes watched my mouth. "You like it? Me calling you that?"

"Yeah," I admitted. As my mind summoned the sensation, my cock ached.

Christ.

"I like hearing Taro from you."

I smirked. "Yeah?"

"Yes."

I traced a couple of fingers over his shoulder, his arm, and back up again to circle them over his chest. I laughed to myself.

"What?" he asked.

"Just didn't know I'd be where I am now and gettin' hard over it too."

Taro's smile widened, and he started laughing, rolling to his back. I watched him. I could do so now, freely. Though shyness slipped in, and my face burned as once more nerves flickered to life. My gut acted up when he rolled back to face me.

Swiftly, Taro pushed me to my back and straddled my waist. My heart thumped hard in my chest as he pushed up my top.

"I had hoped, but I didn't think *you* would be here in my room wanting to 'talk' after that kiss we shared." His hands paused from pushing up my Henley. "You did come in here for something?" He groaned, closing his eyes. "I didn't force myself—"

"No," I said quickly. "I wanted to— Christ, this is embarrassing."

His grin slipped back in place as he tugged at my top. I lifted enough for Taro to helpfully remove it from my body. He bit his bottom lip, looking down at me. "What's embarrassing?" he asked.

"This. I don't know. I wanted to taste you."

His eyes fluttered closed. "Josh."

Reaching up, I cupped the side of his neck and

pulled him down to have his mouth. To claim it. He rocked over my hardness, and I pushed up to match his rhythm.

I didn't care any longer.

This, being with Taro, having him in my arms, was a wild ride, and the feeling was a high I didn't want to give up yet.

It felt good.

Right. In my head, chest, and body.

The man made me harder than a damn drumstick.

His lips trailed down my chin, my cheek, my neck. I wanted to sink into his skin and feel this forever.

Jesus Christ. Mind blown.

Taro kissed down my chest and licked at my nipple before biting. I hissed out a breath and rubbed my hands up and down his skin, his arms, back, head, then fingers through his hair. He kissed down further, where he was trying to head clear, but it wasn't the time for it.

I had to laugh at myself, because I didn't know where the fuck I had gone.

I loved sex.

I could fuck day and night for that sweet release, yet here I was, holding back because, and fuck me for thinking it, I wanted to know him.

Yet did he want that from me, or was he only after one thing?

Shit, did he want a one-night stand?

Taro paused at the top of my pants and lifted up. "What's wrong?"

"What?"

"You tensed up."

Shit, fuck, shit. What did I do? What did I say? Something where I didn't sound like a moron with a crush?

A crush. I'd never had one before.

Taro lay over me, folding his hands on my chest to rest his chin on them. Waiting for me to say something. I didn't know what to say though.

Instead, I brushed his hair away from his eyes and ran my gaze over his face.

What was it about this that had me fucking weak in the knees?

"Like your hair colour," I said softly.

He flashed me his teeth in a grin. "Good to know."

When I started running my fingers through his hair and watching it drop from my grasp, only to do it over again, his eyes drifted closed. How did a guy have such soft hair? A small smile touched his lips, his head tipped to the side, cheek resting on my chest. I could play with his hair all damn day long.

My heart thundered. Could he hear it?

He rubbed his head against my chest, and I wrapped my other arm around his shoulders, holding him to me. His weight settled in more. He wasn't heavy. He fit perfectly. I liked the pressure of having him on top of me.

I squeezed my eyes shut while continuing to play with his hair.

Why did this work for me?

Eventually, his breathing evened out, and I relaxed more into the bed by putting both arms around his body. Holding him. I didn't hold anyone in bed. Not like this.

Sleep started to drag me under, and all I could think was that I'd lost the will to fight this. I wanted to take that chance.

CHAPTER TWELVE

WOLF

$\mathcal{I}$ had never slept as soundly as I had last night. It was all to do with the man curled into my back with his nose buried in my hair. A smile overtook me. I had thought he would have run after he had tensed up. He hadn't. He'd *played* with my hair, touched me, held me like he wanted to do that more than anything else, more than I thought he would.

I couldn't believe I had fallen asleep on him, and he'd stayed.

It meant something, didn't it?

Josh liked me. That sounded juvenile, but I was sure it was true.

Josh.

Not Ruin.

It was good to call him by his real name. To me, it meant a lot, just like when he used my name. It was a connection we hadn't had before.

His arm around my waist tightened as he stretched and made a noise in the back of his throat. My cock responded.

A knock sounded on the door, and Josh woke with a start, cursing. He leaped over my body and landed on the floor with a thud.

"Wolf?" Ryo called because of the sound. Before I could stop Ryo, he had the door open and stood in it, looking around frantically with a gun pointed. "What's going on?"

Tension slapped at me. Would Josh stay hidden? Would he want no one to know? I could understand why, but annoyance didn't begin to describe my reaction if that was the case.

"I—"

"Nothin'" came from the floor before Josh stood with his hands on his waist. He glared from Ryo down to me, then back to Ryo. When his gaze dropped to me once more, it ran over my body, and his eyes narrowed even more. He moved quickly and picked up the sheet to wrap around me, covering half of my head as well.

My breath caught in my throat. Was he seriously hiding me from Ryo's gaze?

Ryo snorted out a laugh before he covered it with a cough.

"Can I help you, Ryo?" I asked and tried to slap the sheet away, but Josh held it in place.

My chest expanded at the thought of Josh being possessive, but it was only Ryo.

"You were late," Ryo said.

"What time is it?" I tried to pull the sheet away again, but Josh sank to the bed behind me and held it in place. "What are you doing?" I demanded.

"Nothin'," he clipped.

"It's after eight, Wolf," Ryo called.

"I'll be out soon," I told him.

"Very well. Ruin, I also closed your bedroom door, since you left it open sometime through the night."

Ruin grunted. "Thanks."

Ryo laughed again before I heard the door close. Josh's hold on the sheet loosened, and I thrashed my hands around until the sheet dropped off my head, pooling around my waist. I went to turn until Josh tugged my back into his chest, and his lips met my shoulders.

"Sorry," he offered sheepishly.

"What was that?" I asked.

"I panicked."

"Panicked? Not over being seen in my room, but over Ryo seeing me half-naked?"

My pulse raced even before he answered with "Yeah. I didn't like the thought of anyone seein' you like that."

"I could have felt the same way, with me not wanting him to see you like that," I pointed out.

"I thought that too. It's why I sat behind you."

I couldn't help it. I laughed. He was crazy, but I liked it.

With another surprising kiss to my neck, he stood. I turned and placed my feet on the floor. I used my hands at the backs of his thighs to tug him between my legs.

I stilled when my emotions bubbled up. Why did I suddenly feel like crying?

It was stupid.

But staring up at what I desired, knowing he had come to me willingly to try this out, meant everything to me. Where had my flirty, confident side gone?

"Hey," Josh uttered, cupping the side of my face.

Pushing the wild emotions back, I smirked up at him. "Morning wood again?"

His chuckle was low. "Yeah, you could say that. Plus, my balls are sweatin' up a storm sleepin' in these pants."

He still had his leather pants on. I snorted. "Thanks for that image, but at least you look good."

His eyes warmed. "Do I?"

Rolling mine, I said, "You know it, pet."

"Pet?"

"Yes, *my* little pet."

"Ain't anythin' little about it."

"Oh, I know. I felt it last night."

He winked, dipped down, and pressed his lips against mine. "Better let you get ready for work, busy man."

I whimpered against his lips. "I don't want to."

It drew another chuckle from him, and I loved hearing it. "Too bad. I promised Mimi we'd go bloody horseback riding." His mouth met mine in another brief kiss, and he started for the door. Was he leaving to get away? Did he regret anything? Would he go back to how he was and tell me to fuck off?

A new pressure clutched at my heart. "Josh," I called, my tone a little higher than normal.

He turned. "Yeah?"

"I'll see you tonight?" *Please don't run. Don't listen to your inner demons saying this is wrong. Please like me.* Yes, my confidence had walked out onto the balcony and taken a jump off, fearing losing what I had gained. The thought twisted my stomach into knots. Already Josh was something important to me, and I was all mixed up within myself. I didn't know how to act or what to do to make sure I could keep him at my side.

His smile was big and bright. "I'll be seein' you, Taro."

The pressure eased. "Have fun," I told Josh, still wanting him to stay.

"You also," he teased, and I glared. But it faded as soon as he was out of the room, closing the door behind him.

"My God," I breathed, and slapped a hand over my mouth. A thrill ran up my spine. Josh came to my room with his own free will. I may have started the kiss, but he knew what he was doing and who he was doing it with.

It shocked me we didn't go further than making out like some horny teenage boys, but I also liked the fact we hadn't. I was used to being used for my position in the family. I was used to being wanted for money and the lifestyle.

I had never been treated as I had the previous night, like Josh had done.

No one had wanted to only kiss me, hold me, be with me without an ulterior motive.

What was that man doing to me?

One night and I felt... excited, giddy, overwhelmed, but in a good way.

Though, what happened if it all ended because this wasn't what Josh wanted? Because *I* wasn't what Josh wanted.

I was a guy after all, and he'd never been with one. *That* I was sure of.

Standing, I shook my head and made my way to the bathroom. I refused to think about the what-ifs. I would enjoy what we had, even if it lasted for just now. There wasn't a chance in hell I would miss having a piece of Josh. I could only hope my confidence would return and I'd stop worrying to the point I second-guessed myself.

Ruin

MIMI BUMPED her shoulder into mine as we made our way back to the house after a ride, which wasn't too bad considering it had been on a horse and not my bike.

"What?" I asked.

"You seem happier this morning," she commented with a smile.

I shrugged. "Good ride, good company, got nothin' to complain about."

She snorted and rolled her eyes. "Really? There's nothing else that's made you happy?"

I ruffled her hair, which she scowled at. "I'm always in a good mood. Nothin' new there." Except for the fact I'd slept like a baby beside a guy I had a goddamn major crush on. If I hadn't walked out of his room this morning, I would have taken things further. That was why I bolted quickly. He'd taken my damn breath away with the morning light shining in from the balcony window. Right before I hid him under some blankets. I still couldn't believe I acted like that, but shit, I'd hated having another guy seeing Taro that way. Half-naked, hair rumpled, eyes hooded from sleep.

"And you're spacing out with a weird little smile on your face," she accused, moving to stop in front of me with her hands on her hips.

"What do you want, Mimi?" I asked, amused.

She slapped my stomach. "We're friends. We tell each other things now. Like, say, I don't know, the fact you slept in my brother's room."

"Okay, I slept in Wolf's room." She didn't need the little details of how I called him by his first name. That was for me.

"You're a pain in the butt. What happened?"

"You do know that even though I kissed a dude, I'm

still a guy, and I don't do this woman-gossip session, right?"

She beamed at me. "You two kissed?"

I groaned and gently shoved her out of the way, starting for the house again. With a laugh, she strode to catch up. "How was it? Your first kiss from a guy."

"Mimi," I whined. "Shut it."

"No way. This is too juicy. Ruin, the man-whore member who only does women, has been kissed by a man. *My* brother." She clapped. "This is awesome."

Snorting, I stared down at her as she rambled on. She looked at ease. Happy even. She had been this way in Ballarat, but she was also different back home. Shy. Quiet. Here she wasn't. Would she stay on after her dad died? Whatever she decided, I'd stick by her choice, but I knew one thing. Melbourne wasn't for me. Ballarat was my pace of things.

So what did that mean for Taro and me?

Shaking my head, I pushed that thought away. I was going to live in the moment, and right then, my gut needed some food in it.

"I can't believe you're not telling me anything."

"How did you know I was in there anyway?"

"You left your door open, dingbat."

"I could have gotten up early and gone for a walk."

She shook her head. "You would have told me if you were going far." She bumped into me again, easily showing affection. "You're a good friend like that."

She did seem cool that I slept in her brother's room,

but wasn't it weird for her also? I didn't want her to feel uncomfortable.

"Mimi," I said.

"Yes?"

"Ain't it weird knowin' I was in your brother's room after we—"

"Let's not speak of that. It was a one-night slip-up from me when I thought I'd lose the company I had and the safe place. I promise I'm okay with whatever happens. I wish you both luck because you're both pains in the butt."

I curled an arm around her shoulder and tugged her close, kissing her temple. "You're a good chick, Mimi. Cowboy's a lucky guy to have you."

Her cheeks pinked. "He doesn't have me."

"But you want him to?"

"No… I don't know…. We've been texting."

"Textin's good. Get to know one another."

"I do miss him," she admitted softly.

"Honey, if you want him here, I'm sure he'd come."

She shook her head. "It's too much of a hassle."

"I don't think he'd see it that way. He'd be honoured to be here for you."

"Hmm, maybe," she mumbled, biting her bottom lip. "I'll see."

I smiled. I hadn't realised how serious it was with Cowboy, since she'd held so much annoyance for me. Then again, it could have also been because I made her feel like an idiot in front of the brothers when I announced there'd be nothing more between us. Although, I guess it worked out if Cowboy and Mimi were getting closer. I hoped it did because Cowboy would be good for her. He was a great guy. At first, I was surprised he joined Hawks, but I'd found out his foster dad was a dick, and Cowboy wanted an out. Hawks gave him that, and we took care of the foster dad. The guy had talent in making signs and worked hard at Coyote's shop.

Yeah, he'd be good for Mimi, if she rocked up back to Ballarat with me. Though here wasn't too far from Ballarat; a couple of hours' drive.

Letting that sink in helped me ease the slight fear I had for when I returned without Taro.

Christ, this "feeling" shit is happening too fast.

CHAPTER THIRTEEN

WOLF

*D*ead on my feet, I dragged myself up the stairs and down the hall to my bedroom. It was late. I glanced at Josh's door, hoping it was open or he would step out. There wasn't the chance to see him earlier, since Jiro had attempted to take his daughters back. It hadn't worked, of course. There were too many people backing me in the changes I was making within the family.

I lingered for a moment, debating if I should wake Josh.

I wanted to see him.

He'd been on my mind all day.

His kiss. His hands. His body.

All of him.

Still, I couldn't bring myself to walk to his door and knock. The worry of him rejecting me was too fierce, specifically that he'd come to his senses and pick women over me. I still couldn't believe my luck last night.

Fisting my hands, I ground my teeth together and thought, *Screw it.* He was what I wanted, and I would make sure he knew it in one form or another. I would walk into his room and demand his attention liked the starved man I was for him.

As soon as I freshened up a little.

I pushed open my door. The moonlight shone through the window from the balcony, and it was then I saw a shape in my bed.

My heart skipped a beat.

No other would be foolish enough to enter my room without speaking to me first. Especially if they made themselves at home by climbing into my bed.

No other than the tattooed man I wanted. It seemed I didn't need to seek him out, which sent a wave of pleasure through my body.

The sheet was pooled around Josh's waist as he lay on his back. My throat thickened with emotions at seeing him there.

He'd come to me.

He'd wanted to see me as much as I had him.

He'd picked me.

He hadn't let his fears and worries contain him.

I stripped out of my shirt, pants, and socks. Freshening up could wait; I needed to have him in my arms. I ached for it.

I made my way over to the bed and paused, staring down at the beautiful man before me. My cock ached. He was stunning.

"You gonna stare at me all night like a creep or get into bed?"

I couldn't contain my smile. "Stare at you."

He snorted, reached out, and dragged me down on top of him. "Hey," he whispered, cupping my neck.

My pulse raced. "Hi. You're here."

"Hope that's okay?"

"It is."

He tipped his chin up. "Good."

He was there. Right in front of me, and all I could do was stare at his eyes, his lips, cheeks, chin, hair. My heart couldn't take it.

He'd been all about women, yet he was taking a chance on our attraction.

"Taro," he uttered, threading his fingers into my hair.

I dipped my head and took his mouth. It started out light, a peck or two before his lips, his scent, got to me —that, and how he'd tightened his hold on me. I snuck my tongue in, but he was just as eager to get a taste. His arm wound around my waist and gripped me to him as the heat of the kiss intensified. I spread my legs, straddling his waist, feeling his erection through the thin sheet and our boxers. I rubbed against his hardness, drawing a moan from deep within him.

Smoothly, Josh rolled us so he was on top, his hand at my throat. A dark look slipped into his eyes as he gazed down at me. The hold was tight, but not enough it broke off my panted gasps.

"Fuck," Josh clipped when he rocked against my own hardness.

I ran my hands up and down his arms, waiting to see what he wanted. I would give him anything.

I would.

Why did that thought scare me?

Why was he different from any other I had been with?

He didn't care who I was or what I had; he was here to test this connection between us. Just us, not for anything else.

When he rocked his hips into mine, I bit down on my bottom lip, and he groaned. My cock pulsated. I wanted him inside me. I hadn't done that in years, given myself over freely. While I took, I wanted to give with him. I wanted him to fuck me.

"Josh," I breathed.

The simple breathy word seemed to undo him. He kissed me with everything he had, and I took it all, wanting him, wanting everything. But I needed more. I tugged his boxers over his hips as he ground up and down over me, lost in the kiss. I lowered my boxers enough to slip a hand between us and grip our dicks together.

"Fuckin' Christ," Josh bit out against my lips before connecting our mouths in another hot and heavy kiss.

I jerked my hand up and down both of us, already so close to losing it because this was Josh. It was his body over me. His dick in my hand. His mouth on mine.

Josh ground down. Breaking the kiss, he pressed his hands on either side of my head and gazed at where I pumped both our cocks.

"So good," he uttered, pressing his forehead into my shoulder where he bit my neck. "Taro, fuck, close."

"Yes," I panted. "Me too."

"Jesus," he snarled, lifting up enough to watch my hand rub up and down over our lengths. "Wanna see."

"What?" I asked, my pulse in my throat, my gut tightening.

His heated, hooded eyes met mine. "Wanna see our cum together on your skin."

My lips parted, a moan slipping free, his words hitting me right where I needed them to. "Josh," I whispered, pushing my head back into the pillow as my cum shot out over my stomach.

"Fuck, fuck," Josh grunted. His gaze was down on our dicks, on my stomach, and then I felt more fluid join mine as I looked down to see the tension tightening in Josh's arms, his neck, and his chest as he came.

Beautiful.

Stunning.

Amazingly mine.

He let out a ragged breath. Without a care to the stickiness, he leaned down and led me into a passionate kiss before breaking it with a final peck. "Didn't know it could be like that," he said softly and slipped off the bed, walking over to the bathroom.

"Like what?" I called, lifting to my elbows to watch him.

He didn't answer until he was back out of the bathroom with a damp washcloth. His smile caused my stomach to tingle. "Didn't know comin' like that with a guy could be damn good."

I glared. "I'm glad you didn't know." Not knowing meant he hadn't shared this with someone else.

Josh chuckled. My eyes widened when he sat on the edge of the bed and cleaned up my stomach. There went my organ in my chest again.

"Means I liked it, Taro."

"I know," I said, watching his hand.

He flicked my forehead. "Cocky."

I blinked. "Sorry, I didn't mean it to sound like that. I'm…." Dear God, my cheeks heated even before Josh dropped the cloth to the floor and ran the back of his fingers over my cheek. I turned my head away, unable to take the sweetness. I wasn't used to it. "Anyway, can we get some sleep?"

Josh snorted. "Sure. Want me to leave you to it?"

"No," I said too quickly.

Josh grinned. "Thought so." When he lifted the blanket, I scooted over, giving him enough room. He took it and more. He pressed up close to me and twisted me so he could become the bigger spoon.

"How was your day?" he asked.

My body went haywire—in my chest, my blood, my

stomach. Not to be outdone, my emotions also flickered to a higher heat.

How was he perfect?

How could he act as if this was normal, especially for him, when it should be way out of his comfort zone?

I couldn't understand him.

"Taro?"

"Oh, um, long and boring."

"I heard Jiro was causin' shit. Was gonna head over to help, but before I could, I was told you had it sorted."

I nodded, biting my bottom lip. Josh would have come to help me because he wanted to. He wasn't expected to. I didn't pay him. He just *wanted* to. "He's nothing I can't handle."

"Yeah, I'm understandin' that." Josh kissed my shoulder. "Mimi knows I was in here last night and saw me come in here tonight. You cool with that?"

Dear God, this man would kill me.

"Are *you?*"

"Yeah, Taro."

"Then I am."

"Good."

Wanting to hear his voice more, wanting to know him, I asked, "Where did the name Ruin come from?"

Josh snorted. "The prez gave it to me when I was fully patched in as a member. This was after I ruined my first ride and cried about it."

Smiling, I told him, "That's cute."

He nipped at my shoulder. "It ain't cute; it's manly.

Only a real man would cry over their baby gettin' ruined."

I hummed under my breath and got another nip to the shoulder. I gripped his arm around my upper waist and asked, "Do you have any siblings?"

"I do, two sisters. One's a couple of years older than me, the other younger. Had a shit dad until I was in my early teens. Lucky he died and then Stoke came along."

"Stoke?"

"A brother from Hawks. Older. My dead dad had been a part of Hawks, but we never got involved with the MC until he died. They came in, took care of some family shit for us, and then Mum and Stoke hit it off. Thank fuck."

"You sound proud of him."

"Proud to call him a brother and also a dad. He's a good guy. The best."

"I'm glad you have that. Does your sister have someone?"

"Yeah, another brother. He was a dick to start with but got his act together when Nary went through.... Fuck, she was kidnapped, abused, and messed up. Vicious made sure to be by her side after it and has never left."

Nausea twisted in my gut. "I'm sorry your sister went through that."

"Me too. She's good now though."

Unsure what to say, I nodded. Josh's life hadn't been what I thought it would have. I knew I wasn't the only one to walk through hell when it came to their own father but hearing it from someone I cared for was harder than I expected it to be.

Like I had with my father, my uncles, and all the elders who had put the women through something vile, I wanted whoever had hurt Josh's sister to pay.

"Hey," Josh whispered against my shoulder with another kiss. "What are you thinkin'?"

"Is he dead? If not, I will help kill him."

Josh stilled at my back. His arm tightened around me as he dragged his nose from my neck into my hair. "He's gone. We made him pay. That's what Hawks does. Protect our own in any way we can. Even if it comes to killin'."

Pride swelled inside of me. "When everything is in order in the family, it is how I will run this family."

"Speakin' of runnin' the family, you should get some sleep before you're wrecked for tomorrow."

"I suppose you're right."

"Babe, I'm always right, just remember that."

My heart stumbled. "I don't think I will, pet."

He chuckled at my back, and it felt like my body was floating. I had never experienced this before and wanted to keep the content bubble Josh provided, but fear gripped my stomach—if I did lose this happiness, what would that mean?

CHAPTER FOURTEEN

RUIN

a few nights later, a knock sounded on Taro's door. He was still sound asleep, so I climbed out of bed to answer it. Ryo stood with a grim expression. "It's time," he said.

"Fuck," I muttered. "I'll wake him, and we'll get Mimi."

Ryo nodded and moved across the hall to lean and wait. I closed the door, turmoil fluttering inside me. I hated this for Taro and Mimi. Hated their dad was a motherfucker, but most of all that he was about to die and they would feel it.

I strode back to the bed, unsure just how much time their dad had. Crouching beside him, I gently shook his shoulder. "Taro?"

He groaned. "Later, tired."

I couldn't believe I was smiling at a time like this, but fuck, he was cute. "Babe, come on, it's your dad."

His eyes flew open. He sat bolt upright and flicked the sheet away. I moved aside when he climbed out. We both dressed quietly. I slipped my phone into my back pocket but also bent to take out my gun. I wouldn't go unprotected in a vulnerable situation. Taro may have his guards, but I'd be sure to have his and Mimi's back. Worry had me dipping my brows when Taro started for the door without me.

I reached out, taking his arm. "Hey."

"I have to get to Mimi and Mother."

I tugged him into a hug. "I know. *We* will. Here for you, Taro."

He nodded against my chest, taking a deep breath. I dropped my hold and together we made our way out of the room to Mimi's. I knocked before opening the door. Mimi sat up quickly, rubbing her eyes.

"Dad?" she whispered.

"Yeah, honey," I said when Taro didn't reply.

Once out of bed, she pulled on a sweater over her pyjamas. She met us at the door and took her brother's hand. Together, they walked down the hall while Ryo and I followed.

I didn't know where they needed me, but I would be here for them through it all. I'd do anything for either of them.

This fucking sucked.

The house was quiet, with the majority of the occupants still sleeping. The atmosphere sombre. We turned a corner and reached the guards standing outside the closed door to their father's suite. A guard opened the door to the room. I stopped, as did Ryo.

Mimi and Taro looked back at me.

"I'll be right here," I told them both.

Mimi gave me a watery smile, and Taro nodded. The door closed, and I leaned against the far wall.

"They'll be all right," Ryo said.

"Yeah, eventually." I glanced at Ryo before I shifted closer. He gave me a weird look, but I didn't want anyone to overhear what I was about to say. "Look, what do you think of me inviting a brother here for Mimi? They've been gettin' close, and I know she's got feelin's for him. Do you think that she'd want it, now?"

The thought had come to me as we walked down the hall, but I wasn't sure if it was a selfish act or not. I wanted to be there for both of them, but Taro more. I felt like a complete cunt for thinking it. I didn't want to brush Mimi aside since she meant a lot to me.

"Forget it," I said, sure I was being an arsehole for even thinking it.

"I think she would need this boy's support if they truly were getting close."

Shit.

Now I didn't know what to do.

"Should I call him? Find out first? I ain't leavin' Mimi to grieve on her own so I can take care of—" Ryo's hand landed on my shoulder.

"It shows you care for them both. Mimi won't hold

any action you take against you. She understands what you and Taro have. She will also understand your wanting to take care of him. Call your friend. We will all be there for them when they need us."

I nodded. "Yeah, all right, I'll do it." I moved off down the hall a little, with Botan following. I hadn't even seen him rock up. Did the guy never sleep? Shaking my head, I pulled out my phone and looked through for Cowboy's number. After pressing against his name, I held my phone to my ear.

"Ruin? Everything okay? Is it Mimi?" And that was all I needed to hear. This choice was the right one because he was worried about her.

"Brother, her dad got worse. Heard you two were close. Could be good you came."

"On my way. Text me the address."

"Will do," I answered before he hung up. I quickly texted him and moved back to stand beside Ryo. I didn't know how long we'd wait, but no matter how much time went by, I'd stay here for them.

A MAID STOPPED in front of me with a tray. I took a coffee and muttered my thanks before she moved on. A couple of hours had gone by, enough for Ryo to send Botan to retrieve Cowboy from the front entrance. Footsteps approached. Cowboy followed Botan with a grim face. He wore jeans, cut, and jacket, and when he saw me, his chin lifted in greeting. I handed my mug to

Ryo and approached. We hugged, slapping each other's backs.

"Thanks for comin', brother."

"Anythin' for Mimi," he said, and when we pulled apart, I saw a red tinge to his cheeks.

I dropped a hand to his shoulder and nodded. "Good."

His brows dipped. "I didn't think you'd reach out after—"

"Cowboy, Mimi and I are *friends*. I was a dick back then, but she's forgiven me. I hated that I didn't see her underlying reasons to reach out to me; instead, I brushed her off. But you've been there for her. You deserve to be here for her now also."

"I'm glad you called."

"Glad to have you here, brother. Come take a spot on the wall. Want a coffee?" I asked just as a cry filled the area.

Fuck.

It had happened.

I moved over near Ryo. We shared a look but stayed quiet. Now wasn't the time for anything but being there for the family. The door opened, and Mimi ran out, searching through the people standing around. I straightened, as did Cowboy. She saw me, but then her gaze locked on Cowboy. Her face crumbled just before she barrelled into Cowboy with a sob. He wrapped his arms around her, one at the back of her head, the other around her shoulders.

"Darlin'," he whispered. "I'm so sorry."

Placing my hand on her back, I rubbed it up and down. "Always here for you, Mimi," I said softly against her temple.

"T-Thank you, Ruin, a-and for bringing him here."

A woman stepped up. "I shall escort you to Mimi's suite."

Cowboy nodded. But his eyes shot to the bedroom doorway. I looked and found Taro blankly staring out at nothing.

"Taro?" Mimi called.

He blinked. "Mother wants to be left alone for a while."

"Is Aunty staying in with her?"

"Yes." He cleared his throat. "Ryo, are things prepared?"

"Yes, Wolf."

"All right." He nodded. "I'll need to speak with the other family members. Have a meeting organised as soon as possible."

"Of course, Wolf."

"Taro," I called.

His gaze flicked over me and went back to Ryo.

No.

Fuck no.

I took the steps to stand in front of him and cupped the side of his neck. "All that shit can wait. Take a moment for yourself."

He glared. "I don't need a moment. I have waited for this day for a long time. I need to move on from it."

"No," I stated.

His hands hit my gut, and he pushed at me. "You do not get to tell me what to do," he snarled.

"Cowboy, get Mimi to her room. If you two need anythin', I'll be a couple of doors down to the left. Ryo, set up a meetin' in a few hours," I ordered while holding Taro's scowl. Cowboy guided Mimi down the hall and away from this shit.

I knew Taro was hurting. Even though he hated the man, he was hurting, and he needed time to deal with it.

"Ryo, if you move, I will fire you." Taro stepped to the side of me. "You came here for Mimi. Be there for her. I do not need your assistance."

I clenched my jaw. "I came here for Mimi, but now I'm also here for you. Don't push me away, Taro. I get it. I know you're hurtin'—"

He snorted. "You know nothing."

"I fuckin' do," I snapped. His jaw clenched, nostrils flaring. We'd talked and goddamn talked a lot recently, getting to know one another. Even when he refused to admit he was hurting, I knew differently. It still did because he had a heart. He cared. He was a good person. If he wasn't, he wouldn't be making the changes within the family as he had. I took a breath. "Taro," I whispered, tugging him into my arms.

His hands gripped at my tee, yet he remained stiff, even with his forehead pressed to my chest.

"Come with me," I told him. I took his hand in mine and nodded to Ryo, who returned it before he went the other way. I led Taro back to his room. He didn't say a word, and when I glanced at him, he stared down at our clasped hands.

I closed the door in the room, and Taro walked off towards the balcony, pulling the door open with harsh movements. He stomped over to the railing and gripped the wrought iron as I stepped out after him. His head dropped, chin near his chest, and I witnessed his shoulders shifting up and down quickly with his fast breaths.

"Taro," I uttered, resting my hands to his waist.

"I hated him," he said softly.

"I know."

"I hated him with every fibre of me."

I shifted closer, moulding my front to his back. "I know."

"He was a cruel man. A horrid, vile piece of shit."

I hummed under my breath; he needed to get this out.

"I wished I had killed him years ago." He sucked in a ragged breath. "I hated him."

"Babe," I said gently, tucking his hair behind his ear and kissing his neck.

"Fuck," he groaned, the word full of pain. "I hated him, so why do I care?"

Sliding my arms around his waist, I told him, "Because you're a better man than he ever was."

I quickly moved to his side when he bent over, the pain too much. His forehead hit his hands on the railing. A strangled noise caught in his throat. I cupped the back of his neck, letting him know I wasn't going anywhere. His body shook, but he was silent through the tears he allowed to fall.

Clenching my jaw, I rubbed at my stinging eyes. I hated seeing him in pain. Hated he was going through this over a man who didn't deserve his anguish. All I could do was be there for him. Like I knew he would for me.

The connection between us grew every second, minute, hour, and day. It all drew me to one conclusion: I wanted to keep him.

Even after a few days of having him as mine, I didn't want to see a day without him.

He was mine.

CHAPTER FIFTEEN

WOLF

*J*t wasn't protocol, but I no longer cared what my uncles thought. So Ruin walked beside me into the meeting that consisted of close cousins who oversaw the guns and drugs trade for me, and my two uncles. All men, of course.

Even if they hated Ruin was there, he would stay. I needed him close. He was my air in that moment and probably many more to come.

"What is the meaning of this?" Jiro demanded as he stood, his sons at his back. "He should not be in here."

I didn't reply until I was at the head of the table. "I don't have to explain my ways to you, Jiro," I told him. I stayed standing, eyeing the others around me. My cousins, who had moved to Australia because my aunts had wanted a better life for them, didn't waver from my gaze. It was only my uncles who refused to keep my eyes. "As most of you would have heard already, my father passed early this morning. The funeral will take place in three days. I hope you will give the respect to my mother, sister, and me to take those days to mourn his loss."

They didn't need to know, but I had already grieved, so wouldn't need more time. I refused to let any more hurt take hold of me over that man. But my mother would need it. She would want peace until the time came for the funeral without any family dramas arising.

"Kick him out, and I won't cause any trouble," Jiro snarled, crossing his arms over his chest.

"No," I stated. "I am tired of you trying to give me orders, Jiro. This is your last warning."

Jiro laughed. "My last warning?"

"That is what I said."

"Jiro." Akio stood. "Now is not the time. Our brother just passed. Have some respect."

"Respect?" Jiro spat. "The family head should have some respect and not dishonour us by bringing his whore into a *family* meeting."

Josh chuckled beside me as he crossed his arms over his chest.

Jiro's gaze snapped to him. "Get out. Get the fuck out, now."

Josh laughed once again. "You ever think you're against men who like men because deep down you do?"

Shit. If I didn't think Jiro would kill Josh for those

words, I would have laughed, but I feared for Josh's life. I placed a hand on Josh's shoulder, but Jiro pulled a gun before I could say anything.

"No one disrespects me, especially not scum like you."

Josh quickly flicked his arm out, his own gun raised and pointed at Jiro. "I'm gettin' tired of you, old man."

"You cannot shoot me," Jiro said with a smirk.

"He can, if I give him permission to," I added. "But for now, I want everyone to behave. Father just passed; did you have no respect for him?" I demanded.

Jiro ground his teeth together and lowered his weapon. "Your time to rule is coming to an end."

"That a threat?" Josh snarled, clicking off the safety.

I moved my hand down to Josh's arm and squeezed, but he either ignored it or didn't feel it beneath the anger I saw burning in his eyes.

"You better rethink everythin', old man, because it seems you're forgettin' your place and who backs Wolf. Not only does he have his men, but now he has the Hawks MC, and we don't let anyone fuck with us."

My heart gave a hard thunk in my chest. Josh offered his brothers as protection, and I knew he would call them if he thought I wasn't safe. Emotions tightened inside me.

But didn't the fool know I would do the same for him? I would protect him with anything and everything I had. Even from my own family. The Hawks MC was a clean club; my family wasn't. Did he understand that? Did he know that being at my side could make him dirty by association? It was something I needed to make sure he understood.

But then, if I did, would I lose him?

Was it a risk I could take?

The thought of losing him shot fear to my chest and burned.

Jiro spat to the side and then strode from the room, his sons following. It showed he had respected my father enough to not continue this right then. I dropped my hold on Josh and looked to Uncle Akio, who moved around his chair and pushed it in. He dipped his head. "I am sorry for your loss, Wolf."

"Thank you."

He left without another word, his only son following after him. My other cousins stayed until I released them with a remark of speaking about business later. The room quieted until Josh turned to me, a stormy expression on his face. "I hate your uncle."

A warm smile lifted my lips. Reaching out, I slid my hand to the side of his neck. "Thank you for looking out for me. He's not very liked by many."

"Good. He's a dick, and I'll always have your back."

Would he though?

While he understood my family dealt with illegal businesses, I wasn't sure if he really comprehended how much trouble that brought to the Takahashi family. There were many out there who wanted the trade we had and would do anything to get it, meaning my life was always at risk. It was why Ryo didn't leave my side unless asked, and I already knew he would be standing outside those doors. He would have heard everything and run in if something happened. I could defend myself easily against the family, but the other people interested in the business would bring many to take me out.

It had happened before, and no doubt it would happen again. I didn't like the thought of Josh being in the middle of my mess when he could get caught up in the crossfire and be harmed.

A storm was coming now that Father had passed. Some competitors would think it the ideal situation to move in and try to take what was ours. I had to be cautious, even more so now.

Maybe the right thing to do was to send Josh away. Not only him, but Mother, my cousins—Jiro's daughters—and Mimi. I needed to make sure they were safe before the thunderclouds hit.

So why did the thought of having Josh leave hurt my heart?

For the first time, I didn't know what to do.

"Hey," Josh uttered, stepping closer to me.

I blinked and met his gaze.

"Where did you just go?" he asked, reading me so well.

Smirking, I shook my head. "Nowhere really."

"What do you need?"

You.

Only you.

The realisation had my eyes widening. I didn't

understand how it happened so quickly, but I was well on my way into falling for Joshua.

"What?" Josh demanded, his hands tightening on my waist.

Shaking my head, I ran my hands down to his stomach and rested my forehead against his chest. "Nothing."

"Taro," he growled in the back of his throat. I loved it.

"Joshua," I replied with a smile.

"Babe, what's goin' on?"

"Honestly, I'm finding everything a lot to take in right at this moment." The family, the business, my father's death, and my feelings for Josh.

"Then don't."

A chuckle fell from me. "If only it was that easy."

"It is. Take today for yourself. No one will think bad of you for it. Shit, every boss has time off. You have people at your back to help you. Let them."

I couldn't remember the last day where I wasn't doing something for the businesses or family. There was still so much to do.

"The funeral's organised, right? Already has been for a long time. Business stuff can wait until after the funeral. Babe, you need this. Let me take care of you."

"How?"

He chuckled. "By telling Ryo to run things while we rest in the bedroom. It's all for you, of course."

Grinning, I lifted my head. "Of course."

"What do you say?"

How could I say no since Josh was right? I could use the time without family and business.

The door opened, and Ryo stuck his head in. "I agree with Ruin," he stated.

Snorting, I rolled my eyes. "I knew you would." Taking Josh's hand, I started towards the door. "All right, I'll take some time, but if anything comes up…."

"I will contact you," Ryo replied.

"Yes." I looked at Josh. "Also, can we go and see my mother and Mimi?"

He smiled. "Yeah, Taro."

Taro. I did love hearing him say my name.

MOTHER HAD BEEN SLEEPING when I checked on her, but she was in good hands with our aunt. She was my mother's sister, after all. When we arrived at Mimi's room, the man I had half noticed before comforting her outside Father's room opened the door. He wore a Hawks MC patch. Seeing it reassured me my sister was in good company. Josh wouldn't have had one of his brothers be here for her without knowing there was something between them.

Though I had thought Mimi was still getting over Josh, so who was this man to her?

"Hey," he whispered with a chin lift.

"Cowboy, this is Taro, Mimi's brother. We're stoppin' in to check on her," Josh explained.

"Nice to meet you officially, but Mimi's havin' a rest

right now," Cowboy said to me before his gaze dropped to our clasped hands. I tried to pull mine away, but Josh held strong.

Wasn't he worried about what his friend would think?

I wanted to look at him, to know what he was thinking, but I didn't. Instead, I replied, "You also. Though, I would like to know how you've become close to my sister."

His face flushed. It was strangely endearing coming from a biker, especially when he stammered, "W-Well... um, you see...."

Josh chuckled. "Cowboy's from Ballarat. They've been gettin' close before Mimi came here."

"Don't worry. I'll take care of her."

"Good. Because I would hate to kill a brother to Ruin," I told him.

Cowboy chuckled, until he looked at both of our straight faces. "Wait, you actually mean that."

Josh sighed. "He does." He pulled our hands up and kissed the back of mine. "But I'll keep him under control."

It was my turn for my cheeks to burn. Josh really didn't care how he acted in front of a brother, even when it was so out of character for him and would shock people who knew him. I heard Cowboy choke on his own saliva, but I couldn't look away from the man beside me.

He really didn't care.

It surprised me to the point of warmth, the sensation attacking my head, heart, and soul in all the good, mushy ways.

"You two…?"

"Yeah, brother. But don't tell anyone, since I haven't."

Cowboy nodded. "Got it."

"Tell Mimi we'll do dinner," I ordered.

"Okay," I heard him say before I dragged Josh towards our room.

Our room.

It was no longer mine. But ours.

Again, how did it happen so fast?

Because he's different from anyone I have been with before.

"Where's the fire?" Josh huffed out a laugh.

Opening the door, I waved off the guards from checking the room and strode in, slamming the door behind us. I wrapped my arms around Josh's neck and kissed him like it would be our last. I pushed everything I felt into the kiss and deepened it, drawing out a moan from the man in my arms. He gripped me tightly around the waist. I never wanted it to end. I could do this every day and night for the rest of my life because his mouth, his body, his heart and soul were made for me.

He was mine.

Mine.

Breaking the kiss, we tried to catch our breaths as we stared into each other's gazes. Josh brushed his fingers through my hair.

"You're fuckin' gorgeous."

Shit. My heart couldn't take any more. It was already full.

But I couldn't lose him.

I couldn't.

If I had to give things up for him, I would. It wouldn't be easy, but he would be worth it.

"What are you thinkin'?"

"That I want to suck your dick."

Several noises dropped from him at the same time, a snort, laugh, and groan. "Jesus, Taro."

Sliding a hand down, I palmed his hardness behind his jeans. I smirked. "Look who's ready."

"I'm not sure—"

"If you deny me this, pet, I'll pout all day long while I go back to work."

Another chuckle left him while he shook his head. "You're crazy."

"Just a little."

He cupped my cheeks. "Taro, you don't have to distract yourself with that. We don't even have to talk. We can sit around and watch stupid shit while doin' nothin'."

I lifted my hands to grip his wrists. "I'm not doing this to distract myself. I want to because you make me feel so much. Selfishly, I want to pleasure you in ways where you'll never want a woman to touch you again, because all you can do is think about me, my mouth, and body."

His grin was wide. "How can I argue with that?"

Smirking, I winked. "You can't, so remove these pesky jeans and sit on the bed."

"Yes, sir." He dipped to brush his lips against mine.

"Oh, pet, I like hearing *sir* from your mouth way too much." He made me happy, lighter than I had ever felt. I would never get enough of him.

Josh chuckled as he walked over to the bed. I stood back and watched when he faced me and undid the top button. He paused.

"Don't be a tease now. My mouth is already watering from thinking of having a taste of you," I told him, my tone huskier than normal, driven by lust.

Josh's eyes heated, his nostrils flaring, desire riding him. Quickly, he slid the zipper down before he pushed his jeans and boxers low and kicked them off. His cock bounced free, already hard and ready for me. I bit my bottom lip, my body heating even more when he pulled his tee from his body.

God, he was beautiful.

Josh sat on the edge of the bed and spread his legs with a wicked grin on his lips.

My heart beat wildly in my chest as I undid the buttons of my shirt while I stepped over to the bedside table and took out the lube, placing it in the pocket of my pants. Josh watched me but said nothing, though I could see the pulse at his throat beat crazily.

I stepped in front of him and bent to capture his lips. His fingers threaded into my hair and gripped. Our mouths attacked, our tongues tangled, and I ran both hands over his warm back, shoulders, then arms. Josh tried to drag me down on top of him, but I broke the kiss and shook my head. Instead, I dropped to my knees between his legs.

My eyes drank him in as I reached out to palm his dick, drawing out a groan and pre-cum at the tip. I licked the latter away and caught Josh's hands clutching the sheets.

"Taro," he uttered.

Peering up at him, I cupped his balls and gently rolled them around before I dipped in and sucked his dick down to the base.

"Fuck," Josh clipped low. He dropped back to an elbow and used his other hand to touch my face, my neck, my hair. Slowly, I grazed my lips up while swirling my tongue around him.

"Christ, Taro. Fuckin' perfect," he muttered, watching me bob up and down on his dick. His stomach muscles contracted and loosened as I went. His hand didn't let up touching me. A moment later, his head dropped back, eyes squeezed tight, as if feeling, enjoying, getting lost in the moment.

Gorgeous.

While sucking him, I took out the tube of lube, opened it, and squirted some onto two fingers. I dropped the tube and touched the slicked-up fingers to Josh's hole. He sucked in a breath and lifted his head, eyes narrowed.

His dick fell free, and I kissed the base as I ran my fingers over his entrance. "Do you trust me?" I asked.

"Yes," he said instantly, which surprised me enough

to freeze. He snorted out a hesitant laugh. "You're surprised?" I nodded. "Babe, if I didn't trust you, I wouldn't be here."

My chest expanded at the knowledge. I kissed his inner thigh, his dick, his hip and then sucked his dick back into my mouth while I gently applied pressure against his hole. Another harsh breath dropped from Josh, and his brows dipped.

"Relax," I said before taking him back into my mouth. I sucked, licked, and ran my mouth up and over him as I edged in some more. He was tight. So fucking tight. I was never used to this much tightness, but I knew I could blow his mind when I reached the right spot.

He tensed, so I made sure to spend more attention on his dick, and soon, he was holding the back of my head, moaning my name.

I pushed in further, and when he cursed, hips near lifting off the bed, I knew I was in the right area.

"What the fuck?" Josh panted.

I licked up his dick and smirked. "Josh, I'd like you to meet your prostate."

When I rubbed over it again, he clamped his top teeth over his bottom lip before groaning, "Holy fuck."

My dick throbbed. Watching him was... such a turn-on. I would be a few pumps from coming.

"Taro," Josh muttered, spreading his legs wider. I withdrew my finger and pushed back in, hitting it again and again. His balls drew up, and he cried, "Fuck. Fucking hell."

Before I could take him in my mouth again, Josh's body tensed. "More," he bit out. I rubbed over the sensitive area, and Josh reached out to snag his hand in my hair as his cum shot out over his stomach. "K-Keep going," he pleaded. I did, and he kept coming.

As soon as his body shuddered with the last drop, I removed my finger and stood. "That was the hottest thing I have ever seen," I told him. Besides myself, no one I had been with before had been able to come from just prostate play—they needed the dick action along with it—but Josh was as sensitive as I was, and I fucking loved it.

As he tried to catch his breath, Josh's arm was thrown over his eyes. I laughed when he gave me a thumbs up.

"I'm going to wash—" Josh sat suddenly, wincing a little, but in the next second, his hands were in my pants, undoing them. "Josh, you don't—"

"Shut it," he ordered and pushed my pants down to the floor. Next, his mouth was on my dick, and he lapped at my pre-cum before drinking me in, taking my dick all the way in his mouth. I grunted around a moan, watching him take me in and out of his luscious lips.

"I'm close," I warned. Josh didn't stop fucking my dick with his mouth. He used his tongue to tease, to drag along all sides of my cock.

"Josh," I cried before I felt my release explode into his mouth. It didn't stop him though. He took it, sucked it down, and searched for more. Josh even used his hand to drag out the last drop before he licked it away.

My chest rose and fell rapidly, both from the sudden orgasm and that it'd been Josh who gave it to me.

"That was quick," he teased with a cheeky smile before kissing my stomach.

I swatted his arm. "Watching you was foreplay for me. I was ready to come in my pants." I gripped the hair on the top of his head and forced his head back. "Did you like it?"

"The arse play or suckin' you off?"

I grinned. "Both?"

His eyes darkened. "Loved it." He dragged me down into a kiss.

I wasn't giving him up.

No matter what, I wanted him by my side, always. I didn't care that it hadn't been long. I knew he was mine.

CHAPTER SIXTEEN

RUIN

*T*he funeral had come and gone. I had been with Taro the whole time, while Cowboy also stayed in Melbourne and hadn't left Mimi's side since arriving. Mimi didn't seem to mind one bit. They looked at each other with stars in their eyes—when Mimi wasn't dragged under by painful thoughts. She seemed to be handling it better than I'd thought she would. It probably had a lot to do with her father being a bastard.

A couple of days after the funeral, Taro and I sat early one morning in the kitchen. It was one of the rare moments he'd sent the guards away. They seemed to be more present than they had been. Them doing so had concern sinking into my gut.

"Taro."

He lifted his eyes from his phone and smiled warmly. "Yes, pet," he purred.

Hearing his name for me brought my own smile forward. I shook my head and asked, "Is there something coming up I should know about?"

Shifting on his stool, his flirty look disappeared. "What do you mean?"

"With all the extra protection gettin' around."

He bit his bottom lip and sighed. "I worry."

My brows shot down, my gut clenching. I'd figured as much, which was why I still carried my gun with me. Still, I wanted Taro to confirm my fears. "About what?"

He smoothed a hand over the counter my way. I took it in both of mine. He licked his lips and stared down at our hands. "You know the types of businesses I handle within the family."

I did. Always had. "Yeah."

He dropped my hand and straightened on the stool. "There are people who want our trade and would do anything to get it. They will see Father's passing as a weakness, use it as an opportunity to take out the main contender in the city. We added extra protection because of the increased threat. If anything happened to Mother, Mimi, the family... you, I...." He shook his head.

"But you're not worried about your life?" I accused, already aware he was that type of guy. He wouldn't care about himself, only others.

Taro smirked and shrugged.

Then I would do it for him. I would protect him.

As I opened my mouth to speak, the windows in the kitchen shattered under gunfire. I was up off my stool, wrapping an arm around Taro's waist and dragging him down to the floor. "Fuck," I clipped when the shots didn't slow. We needed to move, get behind the counter for added protection.

Nothing could happen to Taro.

Fucking nothing.

I took his hand and urged him to move by me. "Stay low. Get around the counter," I ordered as I ran my gaze over him like he was doing to me. I could only see a few cuts and scrapes from the glass shattering over us, but no large wounds. Taro started forward on his hands and knees, looking back once to check that I followed.

Screams started, more gunfire.

Shouts.

One that sounded a lot like Botan. "Get the fuck out of here and live or die here trying to get to our master."

"No. Tell your *master* to come out here."

"He will not speak to the likes of you," Ryo countered.

Taro rested back against the counter with a gun in hand. I crouched in front of him, pulling my gun free, and eyed the doorway. No fucker would get in here for him.

Protect.

Protect.

Protect.

It was the only thing that ran through my mind.

"Who are they?" I whispered over my shoulder, eyes still to the door.

His nostrils flared as he stared at me. "Rivals," he snarled low. "Stay here," he ordered.

I pressed into him before he could move. "No, *you* stay here."

"Josh—"

"Wolf, come out here, or that room won't be the only one we shoot up."

Fuck.

How did they know what room Taro had been in in the first place?

Taro pushed at me, but I didn't move. He wasn't going out there. "Josh," he clipped.

"You are not goin' out there."

"I have to. For my people, my family."

I ground my teeth together. If it was me, I would do the same thing. The thought of him in harm's way soured the taste in my mouth, and an ache formed in my chest.

"Josh," Taro said gently as I heard Ryo trying to stop the situation. I turned enough to see him; his hand rested on my shoulder, where he squeezed. "They need to pay for this. For coming onto the property during our time of grieving."

Drawing in a deep breath, I nodded. "But together."

"Josh—"

"Together, Taro, or not at all." I wasn't giving up on that.

With narrowed eyes, he bit out, "Fine."

"Wait," I called softly. "Can I shoot them?"

His eyes widened before a soft chuckle dropped from his mouth. A mouth I wouldn't mind kissing, except it wasn't the right moment. He shook his head. "Wait until I speak to him, and then we'll see if we need to shoot them."

I winked. "Got it." We crawled out the kitchen and stood in the hallway, heading towards the external door which would lead out to where the stand-off took place.

Before Taro could step outside, I tugged on his arm and moved in front of him, quickly walking outside before him, gun raised.

"Josh," he clipped low.

At least twenty men were facing off against Taro's men, and there were about fifteen of those. Ryo and Botan stood at the front of the group. Taro's men parted, and I led Taro through, shifting the gun to my side with the safety off. I was ready, and if any of the motherfuckers twitched in Taro's direction, I'd shoot even before they talked. I stopped at the front, and Taro stepped up beside me. He held his own gun pointed to the ground.

"Ah, Wolf, it's so good of you to join us. I thought you would have stayed hiding behind your people."

"It's not I who usually does that, Smith. How did you get beyond the gates?" Taro asked.

Smith laughed. "Easily. You should really check who you have within your walls."

"What has Jiro promised you?" Taro demanded.

Anger shot to my gut and warmed me. If Jiro was behind all of this, I'd kill him with my bare fucking hands.

The smirk on Smith's face dimmed a little. The reaction told me enough: that goddamn Jiro was behind this. Smith replaced the smirk and shrugged. "I do not know this Jiro person."

Taro snorted. "You were never good at lying. Tell me what you demand, Smith. I bore of this."

Smith narrowed his eyes. "Do you honestly think you have the upper hand here?"

"I don't think, I know. Hurry up and tell me." It probably wasn't appropriate, but the confidence Taro showed turned me on. He was a good leader, seeming calm and collected. Unlike this Smith guy, whose expression showed every thought.

"Leave this house with your family and no harm will come to you," Smith said.

Taro grinned. "Really?"

"Yes," Smith hissed.

"Now?" I asked.

Ignoring Smith, Taro shot his grin to me. He turned his back on Smith and stepped in front of me. I looked at him but kept notice of what went on behind him. Taro cupped the side of my face before leaning in to press his lips to mine. "Soon, pet," he whispered before pulling back. "So eager to kill. I love it." He patted my chest and faced Smith again, who looked about ready to pop a blood vessel. I rested my free hand on Taro's waist, tugging his body back into mine.

"You disgust me," Smith snarled.

"It wouldn't be the first time, and I'm certain it won't be the last…. Then again, it just might be."

"What do you mean?" he clipped.

"I have my own demand, Smith, before I deal with Jiro."

"What?"

"It's simple, really."

Smith's upper lip raised in a silent snarl. "Tell me then."

"Leave or die. You have five seconds to rethink whatever Jiro has promised you and run before you and your men lose their lives."

Smith laughed. His men were more hesitant but eventually joined in.

"You're delusional. These are not the only men who surround your property. You're outnumbered."

"Am I?" Taro questioned.

"Yes!" Smith yelled and lifted his gun, pointing it directly at Taro. My hand clenched on his stomach, which he patted.

"Five," Taro started.

"Leave," Smith bellowed.

"Four," Taro stated, raising his own gun. We all followed suit.

"You won't win," Smith said.

"And you won't listen, will you?" Taro sighed.

"Jiro, get out here, now!" Smith screamed.

Taro chuckled. "Jiro won't be joining you, Smith. The fool wasn't discreet when meeting with you. We didn't know the plan, but we knew something was coming. I made sure Jiro was watched at all times, and when he started arming himself this morning, he and his family were taken into custody. You're on your own, Smith. Do you still want to do this?"

"You motherfucking—"

"Now!" Taro shouted. In seconds, I stepped from behind Taro, lifted my gun, and started shooting. They tried, even managed to get a few shots off—one caught Botan in the leg—but Smith underestimated Taro. Hell, I didn't even think he had that many men under his command, but there they were, coming from all different places, demolishing the danger in front of us.

Smith hid behind his men like the coward he was, but I saw him aim at Taro. Not realising I'd moved so far from him, I opened my mouth to shout his name, but I needn't have bothered. In the next second, Taro pulled another gun free and shot Smith square in the forehead. The man dropped to the ground, and the gunfire settled.

In the stark silence of the ceasefire, I stalked to Taro, turned him, and searched his body for any wounds. Besides the earlier scrapes, there was nothing. My heart slowed, and I relaxed my shoulders, pulling him into a hug.

He shifted back, brows drawn low, worry filling his gaze. But he shook his head and moved from the embrace to call, "Let's get the injured to the infirmary. Ryo, call the doctor. Mark down if we lost any. We will mourn their deaths and make sure their families will be well cared for. Those who aren't injured, help with the clean-up." He started for the house, and Ryo fell into step beside him.

"Taro," I called.

He didn't look over his shoulder. He didn't stop.

Something was fucking wrong.

I caught up with him just inside. People ran about, helping with whatever they needed. I ignored them and grabbed Taro's arm, turning him towards me.

"What the fuck?" I bit out.

He tugged his arm free. "We'll talk when I'm done." I caught Ryo's wince when Taro went to move off.

"Don't walk away from me," I said, hands clenching at my sides in frustration.

"I have things to do."

"I can help," I told him.

He closed his eyes for a moment, taking a breath. Straightening, he pointed towards a room. "Go and see if Mimi is okay for me, please. I'll meet you in the room."

"I want in on talkin' to Jiro."

"It's a family matter."

That cut. It cut fucking deep. I thought we had something, and we'd be partners, but I was wrong.

No. Fuck it. I wasn't wrong.

He was stressed, and something was eating at him, but he wasn't ready to talk. I wouldn't take what he'd said to heart. I wouldn't. Still, it didn't stop the dull ache in my chest. All I could do was stare at him. If I opened my mouth, I'd say something I didn't mean. With that in mind, I clamped my mouth shut.

Taro looked at me for a while longer before he walked off again. I didn't follow that time. I stayed right where I was as concern twisted my gut.

When I reached Mimi's door, I knocked, and Cowboy called, "Who is it?"

"Ruin."

I heard the door unlock before Cowboy swung it open. I stepped in, my gaze settling on Mimi. "What happened?" she asked. "You've got cuts on you."

"I'm fine. That's nothin'. All I know is that Jiro made a deal with a rival, and it didn't work out the way they expected it. Everyone's safe though."

She let out a shaky breath. "Good." She shook her head. "Goddamn Jiro."

"Who's he?" Cowboy asked. I told him that and what else Jiro had been doing and saying.

Cowboy snarled, "Fuckin' cunt."

"Exactly." I nodded.

"Are you okay?" Mimi asked me.

I moved over to the couch in her room and sank down onto it. Clasping my hands in front of me, I rested my elbows on my knees. "Yeah, fine."

"Is that why you look worried and yet pissed?" she questioned.

"It's nothin', sweetheart."

"Bull, it's my brother. If he's pushed you away, it's because the scene would have worried him. I'm sure whatever he's done or said, he didn't mean it."

"I know." And I did, but... yeah, it fucking hurt he didn't want me at his side after what just happened. I stood. "I'm gonna get in another shower. Probably still got glass and shit all over me." I moved to the door.

"You can stay a while if you want," Cowboy offered.

"I'm good, brother. Thanks, though." I didn't go to Taro's room. I still had clothes in mine, so I headed there, grabbed some new gear, and showered, hoping it'd wash away the depressing thoughts.

It didn't work.

About an hour later, a knock sounded on the door. "Yeah?" I called, standing from the bed.

It opened, and Taro stepped through. I wasn't the only one who'd showered. He closed the door and stepped further into the room.

"Jiro been dealt with?" I asked.

"Yes. He and his sons. The rest of his family have been left with a choice—to leave or stay and follow my rules. They'll be watched closely though."

I nodded, crossing my arms over my chest. I didn't like the distance between us. Why hadn't he walked right over to me?

"I'm sorry for the way I acted before," he started, and my gut tingled in hope.

"Yeah?" I asked since he wasn't offering up any more.

"Yes." He went to the windows and stared out.

"I didn't like being pushed away, Taro," I told him honestly. "Not sure if you were trying to protect me from things, but I need you to know I can take anythin'.

I wouldn't have been out there at your side takin' lives if I couldn't."

He dropped his head. "I know."

"Then what is this? The distance?"

His sad eyes connected with mine. "I need you to take Mimi back to Ballarat."

My brows shot high. "Why?" I demanded.

"There could be other rivals Jiro sought out. Not that he admitted to anything more before he died, but I'm not willing to take a chance and have my family vulnerable."

I scrubbed a hand through my hair and shook my head. "If you're worried about Mimi, Cowboy can take her back."

"No. I don't trust many, but I do you. I want you with her."

A frustrated growl dropped from my lips. "Taro, you're not thinking clearly—"

"I think the separation would do us good as well."

"What the fuck are you talkin' about?"

"You need to make sure this is what you want. You've only ever been with women, Josh. This, what's happened here, could only be a..." He shrugged. "...a lonely moment in time."

"Don't say that bullshit, arsehole. You know it's not only that."

He looked away from my angry gaze. "I worry about my business rubbing off onto the Hawks MC, your family, and causing them problems. The club is clean. *You* are clean. I'm not. You know what I deal in. U-Until

I can clear some things up," his voice wavered, "I need anyone associated to the Hawks MC away from here."

"Clear what things up?"

"Family matters."

I was about to open my mouth and say more when he ate up the space between us and wrapped his arms around me. His forehead hit my shoulder. *"Please*, for me, take this time to make sure you want this. Protect Mimi for me. Mother, my aunt, and Jiro's daughters are going back to Japan for a while. I've spoken to her. It's just for a little while. I... I have so much going on, and I can't handle... I won't be able to handle it if anything happened to anyone I care about. Please, *please* do this for me."

Fuck.

Christ.

"I can help," I tried.

"I know you can, but it's not something I can accept right now." When we didn't know if I was certain I'd still want him. That was what he'd left out.

I rested my head against his and said softly, "What about *your* safety? What about me wanting to stay to protect you?"

His hands pressed into me. "You saw yourself I have many who have my back."

Jesus, he had the right answer to everything, but I still didn't want to leave. I didn't want to give in when it felt like he was.

I understood why Taro struggled, but I wanted to help him. I wanted to stand by his side and take everything on for him. I just didn't know if it would be good or bad in the end.

Did *he* need time to make sure *I* was what he wanted? Or was the fear of losing someone consuming him? I knew he hated his father, but his death so close to this incident wouldn't have helped his thoughts either.

I didn't know what to do, what was right.

I unclenched my teeth, ignored the horrible feeling in my gut, and uttered, "Only for a little while?" *Please don't push me away. Please let me help.* I wanted to say both, but I didn't because he wanted this. He needed this.

He lifted his head, a sad smile touching his lips. "Yes. Very little."

"Fine." I nodded once. I hoped my answer eased some of his tension before he pressed his mouth to mine. He went to pull back, but I wasn't having it. I gripped him to me and deepened the kiss. A promise to him that I still wanted this, that I would give him his time, for now.

CHAPTER SEVENTEEN

RUIN

*T*he ride home gave me a lot to think about. I understood why Taro pushed me to leave. He was under a shitload of stress, and I added to it since he worried about me. Even though he'd asked me to watch over Mimi, both of us knew the brothers would take care of her. Just like I knew Ryo and his men would protect Taro.

But fuck, it scared me to leave his side after what happened.

However, I believed we were strong; we could take on anyone wanting to fuck with us like we already had. Plus, we had good people at our backs, and he *would* be safe. He would, else I'd kick arse if anything happened to him, and that was exactly what I told Ryo before I left. His dry reply had made me smile when he'd said, "It's not like I'm new at this."

There was also the point of Taro wanting me to have time to make sure what I wanted was him. Yes, we'd moved fast in a way and yes, being with a guy was new....

But he was who I wanted. I didn't need time apart to confirm that. I missed him as soon as I left.

His teasing.

His smile.

Him. All of him.

I hadn't even fucked him, yet I already knew he was meant for me. He pissed me off, but there was a high chance I'd do the same to him. We'd work through it.

I'd give him the time he'd asked for.

Only, I didn't know how long I'd last. It already felt wrong being away from him.

In my time away, I'd need to speak with Talon. Taro worried about shit blowing back on the Hawks MC, and I understood his concern, appreciated it even. I would never want any fallout. I'd see what Talon thought, and if it came down to it, I'd step down as a member. The decision was massive and one I didn't take on lightly. However, if I had to pick between Taro and the club, Taro would always be the choice. No one but Taro had captured my attention, left me wanting, *needing* more from them like he had. It didn't mean I wouldn't be a friend to the club. They would always be my family.

When we'd arrived at the compound in Ballarat, I

felt a sense of home. It was good to see the brothers, but I couldn't help but think I wasn't where I was supposed to be. The Hawks were putting on a family barbeque that day, and I looked forward to seeing everyone, but I didn't feel the normal happiness I held when I stood at the bar looking out and around at everyone.

Fuck.

I sucked back the last dregs of my first beer and headed to the exit. I needed to get out of there, maybe catch my family before they left for the family gathering. I'd missed them a shitload, so it'd be good to see them alone before it got too rowdy. The urge to see them had hit me on the ride. I didn't know if it was just because they were my family or if I'd be spilling the beans about a certain someone. I still wasn't sure if I was ready to tell them. Not because I was worried or ashamed. Fuck that. But not having things sorted with Taro, especially not knowing if we had a future, made me unsettled, as did this bullshit of him pushing me away when things got hard for him.

I pushed through the front door and stopped. "Brother and Bakery Girl," I called, spotting Coyote and Channa walking towards the door. I made my way over to them and embraced Coyote first. Christ, it was good to see my brother.

Coyote and I had been close since we were kids. I hadn't realised how much I'd missed the fucker until I actually saw him. I pulled back and smirked down at Channa. I knew my brother would get his crap together and claim this beauty. A blind man could see the chemistry they had right from the start. Of course I gave him shit about it; it was one of my jobs of being his best friend.

"So," I drew out, "he finally manned up and grew some balls to claim you."

"S-Sorry?" Channa asked.

"Yeah, my brother here was pining over you—"

"All right, enough." Coyote glared, but it wasn't at full power. He looked to his woman. "Babe, don't listen to him. Whatever he says is a lie."

With a chuckle, I said, "He's right. Like the fact he's the best rider in the club. See, all lies." Just to taunt my brother some more, I reached out, grabbed Channa's wrist, and spun her so I could place my arm around her shoulders to lead her inside.

"That's my damn woman," Coyote snarled before he clipped me on the back of the head.

Grinning, I complained, "Jesus, brother. I was just being nice and showin' her in."

"Bullshit." He shook his head and wound his arm around Channa's waist; she seemed amused by our actions.

I swept out a hand and bowed. "Lead the way with your wonderful woman." A sudden pang of jealousy had my smile dimming. Coyote could walk in there with his arm around his woman because she hadn't pushed him away.

Shit. I wanted Taro there with me, but was I just being selfish and not taking him and his feelings into account?

I rubbed at the back of my neck, trying to ease some tension, and followed after Coyote and Channa. Coyote glanced over his shoulder and asked, "I thought you were headin' out?"

"Yeah, was just gonna head out for a minute, but it's all good now," I lied, not really in the mood to party. I was worried about Taro. Worried his other uncle would try something, along with his other rivals.

I didn't want to be here.

Maya stepped up and quickly pulled Channa away to meet the other old ladies in the club. Coyote nodded towards the bar. "Come get a drink with me."

With a slap to his back, I said, "Sure, I could use one." I ordered the drinks at the bar and slid one to Coyote, only he wasn't paying attention. His eyes were on his woman. "Shit, brother, you're totally in love."

Coyote smirked. "Never really known what love is. Nothin' like this, at least. So all I'm gonna say is that I think it's damn close."

I knew the feeling. I nudged Coyote's arm and threw out a thought, one that I questioned myself about as well. "Or it could already be there, and you ain't willin' to admit it to a brother before you shared it with your old lady?" I hadn't really admitted anything to Taro either.

I called him mine. Did that mean I loved him?

Maybe.

Dragging myself from my thoughts, I noticed Coyote hadn't said anything about what I'd said. In fact, if I was to guess from the way he stared at Channa, my brother was definitely a goner. Christ, it was good to see; his happiness all but radiated off him. She was his one. Leaning closer, I told him quietly, "You didn't even flinch when I called her your old lady." Chuckling, I added, "I see weddin' bells in the future."

Coyote ignored my taunting and looked at me. "How's bein' back?" We'd been texting since I'd been gone and Coyote knew, like most of the brothers, that I was heading back today, since I'd gotten in contact with them earlier. They didn't know the real reason why yet. Just thought I was back because the job was done. Mimi's dad had died.

Smiling, I shrugged and turned to face the bar, placing my elbows on top so I could grab the beer bottle to play with.

"Brother" was all Coyote said.

Emotions suddenly suffocating me, I clenched my jaw. This past month had been a big one, full of shit that changed everything. Sighing, all I managed to get out was "Fuck, brother."

"Talk to me," Coyote said and kicked my boot.

I drew in a steadying breath. "The whole situation was intense. Fucked up." It had been when it came to Mimi's family and their old rules, the way they treated women. "But...." But then there was Taro.

"You gonna fill me in?" Coyote asked when I said no more.

I didn't want to wreck his night by going over what Mimi had to deal with or my revelation. Straightening, I chugged back the rest of my beer and placed the bottle on the bar before I slapped Coyote on the arm. "Another time. Go enjoy yourself with your woman."

"Ruin—"

I grinned but knew it wasn't a normal one for me. "Nah, brother. It can wait. Seriously."

"Fuckin' bullshit," he clipped as he dropped his bottle to the bar and clasped me on the back of the neck to give me a shake. He always read me too well. Knew I had shit on my mind. "Channa's cool. She won't care if I disappear, but you gotta talk, and we're doin' it. Let's go to my room."

Snorting, I told him, "Bossy bastard, aren't ya?"

Coyote grinned. "Yep." He started off to his room, and I followed. Sweat pooled at the back of my neck. He was a brother I could share anything with. Well, what went down with Mimi and her family, but did I want him to know about me and Taro? I wasn't sure.

He unlocked his door and entered. I slipped in after him and closed the door as a thought occurred to me. I'd never looked at a guy in the way I did with Taro, so I checked my brother out, and all I got from it was that it felt weird to do so. I was man enough to admit he was good-looking, but he definitely wasn't my type.

Not like Taro.

Coyote sat on the edge of the bed and waited. I didn't want to sit. My mind was too busy. Instead, I paced and started explaining things that went down. How fucked Mimi's father and uncles were. How Taro was trying to change things, but it was uncertain everyone would listen, and that there could still be problems.

"Her uncle was going to bargain off his teenage daughters?"

"Yep."

"Fuckin' lucky Wolf put a stop to it."

"My thoughts exactly."

"Seems like he'll be a good leader for the family."

A small smile touched my lips. "Yeah." I nodded. He was the best man to run the family. Already he was changing with the times and protecting those who couldn't protect themselves.

"Still, it's a messed-up situation."

I hummed under my breath. It was, and it would be for a while, but I believed in Taro.

"Ruin," Coyote called.

I faced him, not realising I'd been staring at the wall.

"Is there somethin' else on your mind?"

I quickly shook my head. "Nope."

Coyote sighed and ran his hands down his thighs. "You know you can tell me anythin', right?"

"Yeah, of course, brother."

He eyed me without saying anything more.

Shit. He knew I wasn't being honest.

"You know how our 'rents always go on about how we'll find our one. You think Channa is it for you?"

"I'm close to thinkin' she is. Why?"

I bit the inside of my cheek. Coyote and I were close. He'd always had my back, and I knew he would when I told him.

His eyes widened. "You think you've found yours?"

I scrubbed a hand over my face and moaned. "I reckon."

"Mimi? I always knew there'd be something if you just gave her more of your time."

I huffed out a laugh and shook my head. "She's a great friend, but it ain't her."

"Who?"

My gut tightened. "Wolf," I muttered, keeping his gaze with a straight face, so he knew I wasn't messing around. His head jerked back in shock, his hands lifted, then dropped, and he stood.

"Wolf? As in Mimi's brother?"

"That'd be him."

"You're serious," he stated. I nodded once. His confused face morphed into one of humour right before he started laughing his arse off.

"What the fuck, man?"

"Shit, wait." He waved a hand in my direction, then placed it against his gut while he laughed some more. "Goddamn, the slut of the club fell for a guy."

"Hey," I clipped. "I wasn't a slut."

His laughter settled, and he raised a brow at me.

Grumbling under a breath, I sighed. "Fine, I was active in the bedroom."

He snorted. "Active." He shifted over to me and placed a hand on my shoulder. He shook me. "A guy?"

"Couldn't believe it myself, but the fucker wormed his way under my skin and stayed there."

Dropping his hand, he placed both on his hips,

brows dipped. "Then what are you doin' back here and not there gettin' to know him?"

A "Fuck" slid out before I told him what else went down.

"Let me get this straight. His dad dies, a few days later, the house gets shot up by a rival gang. You guys deal with it, but he's worried about it happening again, so he sends his family and you away?"

I nodded. "He's under a lot of stress, not only from that but his fuckin' family wantin' shit their way or causin' more trouble. It was his uncle who set that whole rival thing in motion, wantin' to get rid of Taro."

"Taro." Coyote grinned. "Does he call you Ruin?"

Glaring, since he'd made me feel like a damn schoolboy with a crush, I clipped, "No. Josh."

"Aww," he teased.

"Fuck off."

"Brother, were you not givin' me and Channa crap before?"

I snorted out a laugh. "That's different. I'm allowed. You really don't care I'm with a dude?"

Coyote rolled his eyes. "Don't ask somethin' stupid. We were both brought up into a family that didn't discriminate when it comes to matters of the damn heart."

Nodding, I added, "Jesus, are we gettin' sappy in our old age?"

Coyote laughed. "Guess we are. But anyway, back to business. What are you gonna do?"

"I don't fuckin' know. He wants time. Do I give it to

him? Let him sort the family and business shit out or go back and support him? Help him?"

I already knew the answer before I even asked. Coyote raised a brow. "I gotta go talk to Talon, then see my family before I head out."

Coyote grinned before he pulled me into a one-armed hug. "Happy for you, brother."

"Thanks. You too."

Who'd have guessed we'd each find the person made for us in a matter of months apart?

TALON HADN'T BEEN in the common room when Coyote and I walked back out. I left Coyote with his old lady and walked down the hall to Talon's office. As soon as I knocked, his gruff voice barked, "Enter."

Opening the door, I stepped in and shut it behind me. "Hey, Prez."

"Ruin, didn't know you were headin' back today."

"Yeah, brought Mimi and Cowboy back. They're in his room if you need to talk to him."

He leaned back in his chair. "Thanks, but is there anythin' new since our calls?"

"Yeah, somethin' else happened."

"Take a seat, brother."

Nerves had my palms sweating as I sat opposite him at his desk. I rubbed them on my jeans. "Early this mornin', a rival gang showed at the Takahashi place and shot out some windows to get Taro—Wolf's attention.

Wolf's uncle planned it, as he doesn't want Wolf to rule the house. It ended in a bloodbath, but Wolf got Mimi, Cowboy, and me out to protect us. He's worried it'll happen again."

Talon leaned forward, elbows to the desk, chin to his hands. "Good of him to think of you lot. Helps Mimi is his sister. What aren't you tellin' me though?"

My throat thickened in fear. I swallowed. "I want to go back."

His brows shot up. "Why?"

Heat hit my cheeks, and I cursed at my reaction. Talon wouldn't care I was into a dude though. "There's somethin' between me and Wolf."

"Somethin'?"

"He's mine," I stated and narrowed my eyes.

He hummed under his breath and sat back in his seat. "You and him together?"

"Sort of." I shook my head. "Yes. Yes, we are. But... he doesn't want to bring any trouble to the Hawks MC."

"And there could be trouble?"

"If this mornin' was anythin' to go by, then yes." He already knew about the uncle and how the family used to run things, how Taro was changing their ways.

"Brother," Talon started as he stood and walked around the desk to sit on it in front of me. "I ain't gonna push you to stop seein' him. If he's yours, then he's yours. Whatever trouble comes, you know we can deal with it. We've got your back through it, and if you're claimin' Wolf, then we got his too. I mean, it'd be good if he stopped dealing in guns and drugs, but if he doesn't, then we'll just make sure the Hawks stays clean and work in the background of things, helpin' out when we can. None of it will stop you from bein' with him."

"I could leave the club—"

"Shut the fuck up. That ain't happenin'. Hawks blood runs through your veins. You're family and always will be, no matter who you're with. Get me?"

A weight lifted off my chest. "Yeah, I get you. Thanks, Prez."

"All I ask is that you keep me updated on things. Call us if you need anythin'. You headin' back today?"

"Gonna go see the family before they rock up here. Not sure how long it'll take. Might head off today or tomorrow mornin'."

Talon smiled. "You happy?"

I grinned. "Yeah, I fuckin' am."

"That's all that matters. The rest we'll deal with when it comes. Now, come on. I better get out there before my woman comes searchin' for me and yells for doin' bookwork on my day off."

"Can't have that."

"Shit no."

Christ, I was damn grateful for the club. Talon's backing meant everything; it meant I could keep my family.

CHAPTER EIGHTEEN

RUIN

*A*t the door to my childhood home, I knocked once before opening it and stepping in, calling, "Mum? Dad?" I only ever used *Dad* when at home. Anywhere else, he was *Stoke* or *brother* out of respect.

"Josh?" Mum cried before she raced into the living room from the kitchen. Tears brimmed her eyes, and she pressed a hand to her mouth.

Smiling, I shook my head. I'd only been gone a month. It was like she hadn't seen me in years. She stalked towards me, her arms opened wide just as Dad stepped into the living room from the bedroom hallway, rolling his eyes at Mum but grinning. Rayne followed him.

"Hey, Ma," I muttered when we wrapped each other

up in a hug. Her breath hiccupped, and her arms squeezed me tighter.

"Josh." Rayne shoved Dad out of the way and ran at me. Mum pulled back in time for Rayne to barrel into me.

"Hey, kid," I said, holding her close. "How's school?"

"Shit," she mumbled.

"Rayne," Mum snapped, wiping at her eyes.

"Rayne," Dad clipped.

"You all swear all the time." Rayne shifted to my side to put her arm around my waist, and I placed mine around her shoulders.

"We're adults, sis," I told her.

"Whatever," she grumbled.

"Good to have you home, son," Dad said before he hauled me into a one-armed hug and pat to the back.

"Good to be back." It was, for now, but I wasn't sticking around for long. It blew my damn mind I'd attached myself to someone so fast, but Dad was right. When you found your one, you just knew.

Damn Taro for making me leave.

"You all right?" Dad asked.

"Yeah, good. Talk to you later about it," I told him, which earned me a chin lift.

"We're heading to the compound soon for a family barbeque. You're going, right?" Mum asked.

"Was just there, caught up with the brothers." I smiled. I didn't say I was heading back there though, because I wasn't sure I would.

Mum studied me a moment. "How about a coffee?"

"That'd be good." I led Rayne into the kitchen, and we took a seat at the table with Dad while Mum busied herself making drinks.

A honk sounded out the front, and Rayne perked up. "That'll be Nary." She bolted from the room, and we all heard the front door being thrown wide.

"What's Nary comin' for?" I asked.

Mum smiled. "She said she'd pick up Rayne for the barbeque since they missed out on her sleeping over at Nary's when Ayra was sick."

A foot to my shin had me cursing and glaring at Dad. "What's up with this?" He waved at my face.

The chair screeched when I pushed back to rub my shin. "What the fuck you talkin' about, old man? You losin' your mind?"

Dad's eyes narrowed as he shook his head. "Cut the crap. Somethin' is goin' on."

"Maybe it had somethin' to do with the shit I'd just come home from, ever think of that?"

He studied me, and it felt like he was looking into my damn soul. "That ain't it."

I snorted. "Yeah, okay," I deadpanned.

"Honey, did something happen?" Mum asked.

Goddamn. They weren't going to drop it.

"Look, all I can say is that Mimi's family is fucked up. Even on his death bed, her dad treated her like shit for not marrying an old man for a business deal. Her uncle was gonna do the same to his daughters if Wolf didn't—"

"There." Dad pointed at me.

I pulled my brows down. "You been smokin' somethin'? Did Killer and Ivy pop over, and you four had another toke party—"

"That was one time," Mum snapped, setting a steamy coffee in front of me and Dad. She glared at me before she went back for hers. "And don't mention that in front of Rayne."

Chuckling, I said, "I won't."

"Hey, hey," Nary called from the front door.

"And then he said he wouldn't come near me because my dad's in the Hawks MC," Rayne told Nary.

I looked to Dad, who smirked. "My job is done."

"If he's scared of Dad, he's not worth it then. You need someone who won't quiver in fear around Dad. Besides, he's a pussycat."

"I am not," Dad yelled. The two girls giggled.

Nary entered first. I got a slap to the back of the head, then a kiss to the temple before she moved around the table to kiss Dad on the cheek.

"Where's Ayra?" I asked.

Nary hugged Mum and explained, "With her dad at the compound. I'm here to pick up Rayne and all her, as Saxon said, 'crap she'll need for just one night.'"

Rayne snorted. "Guess he won't be playing *One Piece* on the Switch with me that *I'm* bringing."

Nary winked at her before she looked at me. "Good to see you're back, bro."

"Miss me?" I asked as Rayne sat next to me.

Nary grinned. "Not in the slightest."

"Bull."

"How did it go in Melbourne? Did you get to see anyone from Hawks?" Nary asked.

"It was okay, and yeah, I caught up with a few." My cock throbbed at the thought of the night I went to the pub and then what happened after in Taro's room.

Fuck. I missed him.

How would he be around my family? I wanted to find out.

"There you go again," Dad said.

Rolling my eyes, I picked up my mug and took a sip. I didn't rise to the bait.

"What?" Nary asked.

Dad pointed at me. "There's somethin' different about your brother."

Everyone stared at me.

Jesus Christ.

"Dad's full of it," I told Nary.

My sister shook her head. "No, now Dad said something, I can see it too."

"He looks tired," Mum added in.

"He stinks," Rayne commented.

I snorted and grabbed Rayne in a headlock, making sure my armpit was right in her face. She squealed and swatted at me.

"Are you dating Mimi now?" Nary asked.

"Gross," Rayne whined, wiping at her face and shoving me.

Laughing, I ruffled her hair. "You love me."

She glared, but I caught her smile. "Apparently I have to because you're my brother."

"See how he's not saying anything about him and Mimi," Nary said.

Sighing, I took another gulp of coffee before saying, "I'm not with Mimi. She and Cowboy are hittin' it off."

"Cowboy?" Mum questioned.

"Yeah, I called him to come down when her dad was... in his last stages. They'd gotten close."

"Poor Mimi," Mum said softly.

"She'll be all right. Better off without him." Nary and I shared a look, probably thinking the same thing—how we were better off without our dad in our lives.

"There's still somethin' different," Dad said, not letting it drop.

"Shouldn't you guys get goin' to the barbeque?" I asked, sucking back the last of my coffee.

Mum suddenly gasped. "You've met someone."

What the fuck? Were my parents mind readers?

I chuckled, then sobered. Maybe this was a part of why Taro sent me away. To see if I'd come out to my family. To show him I wasn't scared of having a man at my side.

"You did," Nary exclaimed.

"Oooh, what's her name?" Rayne asked.

"Is she someone from Mimi's family? Does she have a sister or cousin?" Mum questioned.

"How about we let him talk?" Dad said.

Did I want to tell them? I wasn't going to hide it, but was now a good time to inform them I was interested in a guy?

Rayne nudged me in the side. "Come on, tell us."

"Are we going to meet her?" Nary asked.

"It's still new," I said, my cheeks heating. It was new, but I hoped they would meet him one day.

My gut clenched from nerves. I knew my family would accept this change, but a small part of me worried they wouldn't fully believe me since I'd only had women in my life. Also, it was easier to accept it from outsiders, not someone in their close family.

Sighing, I scrubbed a hand over my face and leaned back in the seat. "But one day, yeah, you'll meet him."

Silence.

All of them wore puzzled expressions.

"Huh? Him?" Rayne questioned.

Nary snorted, then laughed. "Good one, bro."

Mum and Rayne laughed as well, thinking I was joking. Only Dad sat there and stared at me. He knew I was telling the truth, and to prove it to the others, I pulled out my phone and hit a number, putting it on speaker.

"Josh," Taro answered softly.

"Hey, quick question, are we seein' each other?"

He paused, probably confused by my question. "Yes, why?"

"My family didn't believe me," I told him.

"Hang on, wait, let me get this straight…. You rode home, went to your family, and told them about me?"

"Yep. And don't worry, Mimi's safe at the compound with Cowboy."

"I wasn't worried. I knew you would get her there,

but… have you lost your damn mind?" he yelled, which brought a smile to my face.

"How?"

"You don't go away for a month, go home, and just throw this in their faces. You're crazy! They must think I've corrupted you somehow."

I chuckled. "You did."

"*Shut up.* Just shut up. You're lucky I miss you, or I would reach through the phone and throttle you." He missed me. My damn heart soared.

The women giggled around me.

"Josh," Taro whispered, "do you have me on speaker in front of your family?"

Shit, I thought he would have realised.

"Ah, yeah."

He made a noise in the back of his throat, mumbled a few curse words that sounded very threatening to me, and quickly said, "I have to go."

"Taro," I called. I didn't care my family was there. I needed him to know. Needed him to understand that he was on my mind. Even when he pushed me away.

"What?" he snapped.

"Miss you too."

"Josh," he uttered. "Talk soon, you idiot." He quickly ended the call. We would talk soon and face to face. I'd made the wrong choice by leaving. I mean, yeah, it'd been good to see my family and to talk with Talon, but I should have stayed by his side after everything. I'd tell him that and also the fact he wouldn't be able to push me away again as soon as I got my arse back to his side.

He was it.

He was mine.

I knew it before I left, and my certainty cemented when I rode away, leaving a part of myself behind—that part having stayed with the person who was meant for me.

Smiling softly, I glanced up and looked around at my family. The girls were grinning. Mum even had tears in her eyes. Dad wore a smirk. "So, yeah, that was Taro. He's Mimi's brother and runs the Takahashi family."

Dad straightened. "Mimi's brother? The one who gave up his men?"

I nodded. "I've already spoken to Talon about it."

Dad tipped his chin up.

"Hold up." Nary waved a hand in front of her. "Even though I think that phone call is cute, Josh, as far as I know you've only ever been with women. How can you switch it up like that? You can't play with this guy's feelings just for some—"

"Don't," I clipped. "I am not playin' with his feelin's even when it's only been women before him."

More staring happened.

Sighing, I rubbed at the back of my neck. "People change. Like Knife did when he knew he wouldn't want a life without Beast in it. I appreciate you lookin' out for Taro, Nary, but you don't need to."

"Honey," Mum started. "Are you saying you feel like Knife did with this boy?"

Boy. Taro would get a kick out of Mum saying that.

"Yeah." My face heated. "It's still early, but... fuck, he's mine."

"We'll have to meet the guy," Dad said.

"You will," I stated. "Thinkin' of headin' back to Melbourne though."

"Now?" Mum asked. I could see the disappointment in her eyes.

"This is awesome," Rayne blurted. "Now you're into guys, like Uncle Julian is, we can do each other's nails and make-up, go shopping."

"Whoa, hold your horses, kid," I said quickly, chuckling. "It's one guy I'm into, and there's no way in hell we're doin' nails and make-up. I might go shoppin' with you, but I'm still the same person I was before Taro came along."

Rayne rolled her eyes. "Boring. You just shit on my BL dreams."

"Rayne," Dad snapped, but the grin didn't go along with the tone.

"What's BL?" Nary asked.

"Boys' love. It's like a genre in Manga."

"Manga?" Mum asked.

Rayne groaned. "You guys are so old. Graphic novels I read about two guys getting together."

"Are you the right age for these Manga?" Dad asked, and when Rayne looked away, we all knew she wasn't.

"Right, until you reach sixteen, stay away from them," Dad ordered.

"But there are ones for my age."

"Clear it with your mother first so she can check it

out before you look at any more. Where do you even find this stuff?"

"Online."

Dad sighed. "Everythin' is too easy to get online. I mean it, Rayne, check it with Mum. If I find out you haven't, there'll be hell to pay."

"I know."

"Now that's cleared up. Josh, you should come back to the barbeque. I'd love to spend some time with you before you head off. Maybe go in the morning?"

"In other words, Mum's missed you and wants you to stay for a bit longer," Nary supplied what I'd already been thinking.

Nodding, I said, "I can leave in the mornin'." It also gave me more time to talk to Dad and let him know what Talon had said and what had been happening in Melbourne.

One night.

I had to hold off for one night without seeing Taro. I could do it for my family since I'd been stupid enough to leave in the first place.

CHAPTER NINETEEN

RUIN

$\mathcal{A}$ lot of members had crashed at the compound for the night. I took my old room. Nary, though, had taken off with Rayne and Vicious before the party had kicked into the next gear. It ended when a drunken Hell Mouth fell off a table she'd been dancing on for her man Griz; she broke her wrist when she landed on Ivy, another old lady.

It was a good night, though. Always was when it came to the Hawks because every member was family. Even though I enjoyed catching up with everyone, I still felt the urge to leave and get back to Taro. More so now that I was awake.

The conversation I'd had with Dad the night before

ran through my mind. He'd pulled me away from everyone and sat me down at a table out back.

"Spoke to Talon. Know he's already given you the go-ahead. Somethin' I should have said back at the house."

I'd drawn my brows down. "Said what at the house?"

"Should have told you that no matter who you like, you've got our support. Not just the Hawks, but us as your family."

"Dad, I knew you guys wouldn't think less of me because of this."

He'd grunted. "If anyone does say shit, fuck 'em."

Smiling, I'd nodded.

He'd knocked his boot against mine. "You also gotta know, I'm not a fan of this Wolf guy's life. The business he deals in. Only because it could bring danger to you."

"Dad—"

His hand had shot up, silencing me. "But," he added, "I know you can take care of yourself. You seriously goin' back to Melbourne tomorrow?"

"I need to. Told you how I left after that shit happened. I shouldn't have, even when he wanted me to. Taro's gotta understand I ain't backin' away from this. His life."

Dad had grunted again. "I get it, son. It'll be crap to see you go, but know we love you."

My throat had thickened. I'd nodded as I swallowed down the lump of emotions. Even thinking of it now as I lay in bed had me thanking anyone who'd listen from above for my family. It hadn't been smooth sailing, but the shit we'd been through made us come out stronger in the end.

Since I was keen to get on the road and back to Taro, I climbed out of bed and headed for the joined bathroom for a quick shower. I dressed in my usual jeans, long-sleeve Henley, and vest before I slipped into socks and boots. Just when I opened my door to hunt down coffee and food, my phone chimed.

Pulling it free from my back pocket, I saw the name displayed and screwed up my face. Why would Ryo be texting me? My gut dropped, and I quickly opened the message.

Ryo: **I didn't get to speak to you alone before you left, but I am sure Mimi has informed you that Taro didn't mean to push you away.**

A smile tugged my lips up. It was good to see Taro had friends like Ryo who worried about him.

Me: **Figured. Shouldn't have left no matter what he said. I'm coming back today without Mimi so he doesn't worry about her. I've got his back.** I started down the hall towards the kitchen.

Ryo: **Good. He's been in a sour mood. Doesn't help we found out his uncle is staging a coup at the meeting today.**

Anger churned.

Me: **WTF, why? I thought he was the more decent one.**

Ryo: **He's never been decent. The main reason is the power it would bring him. He thinks it's time to**

do something about it since Taro doesn't seem himself after you left.

Fuck texting, I pressed his number and lifted my phone to my ear.

"Ruin," Ryo answered.

"What's Taro gonna do about it?"

"Nothing."

I stopped. "What do you mean nothin'?"

"Right now, he's second-guessing things because he's worried about you."

"What do you mean?"

"We understand where the Hawks MC stands with illegal activity. He doesn't want to cause any problems for you and your family. He's thinking of allowing his uncle to take charge."

"Fuck that," I clipped, stopping in the doorway to the kitchen and glaring at the floor. "He can't do that, Ryo. I spoke to Talon. He's supportive of us, and if shit happens, we'll deal with it when the time comes."

Ryo sighed. "I can only tell him this, but I'm not sure he will believe me. He is looking to step out of those types of dealings down the track, but for now, it will be in his life. I have never seen him torn before."

"Don't let him do anythin'. If the meetin' starts, stall it until I get there. I'll make sure he understands things."

"I'll do what I can," he answered. "Thank you, Ruin. You're good for him."

"And he's good for me. See you soon," I stated, and ended the call. I lifted my gaze and found the kitchen occupied with Talon, Killer, and Blue.

"What's goin' on?" Talon asked.

"Gotta get to Melbourne. Wolf's uncle is staging a coup at the meeting today to take over running the family. Wolf's not gonna do shit because he's worried about me and how Hawks will deal with their business-es." I grabbed a muffin, took a bite, and turned to head outside.

"Hold up," Talon called. I faced him and waited, quickly eating the rest of the muffin to have something in my gut before I left. Talon shared a look with Blue and Killer before taking his phone out to do something with it.

Talon lifted his head, and Blue asked, "We ridin' out?"

"Yep," Talon replied.

"Wait, what?" I asked.

"In-house dramas we can help you deal with. If Wolf's family thinks they can fuck with him, they're wrong. We'll show our support by comin' with you and standin' at his back. Even if it was other shit goin' down with the businesses, we'd help where we could. You guys aren't alone, Ruin. We've got you."

Christ. My chest expanded as the damn fluffy emotions filled my heart.

"You don't have to," I offered.

"Brother, you're family. Prez said you're claimin' Wolf, then he's a part of Hawks also," Blue said.

Killer grunted and lifted his chin my way, also agreeing.

They started forward, moving by me with a grip to

the shoulder. More emotion swirled inside me as I followed after them. We stopped at our rides to check them over. I didn't need petrol or anything, and the others didn't indicate they did either.

A door opened, and Dad stepped out, decked out in his ride gear. He held a bag at his side. He shot me a grin. "We'll pick Vicious up on the way to the highway," he told me.

My throat thickened. This was what family was about. Comradery. "You sure you're up for a ride, old man?"

Dad shot me the finger. "Just try and keep up, Ruin." He dropped the bag and opened it. Guns galore filled the space. "Take one. We're goin' in armed since we don't know if words will get this uncle to back down."

Grinning, I pulled my gun free. "Already got mine. Didn't even think about the rest of you."

"Aww. Stoke, your boy's so worried about his man that he forgot about his brothers," Blue teased with a wink. It was my turn to shoot the middle finger. The brothers chuckled, only to sober when we were all ready to ride out.

I'm coming, Taro.

And there was no way I'd leave his side again. We would deal with everything there was together and see where the future went.

SHOCK RACED through me when we reached Melbourne and the Caroline Springs charter pulled in behind our group. My damn chest was packed to the brim with those cute feelings. I'd always been proud to call myself a member of the Hawks MC, but never more so than then. Their support for me and Taro floored me.

The gates opened to the family estate as soon as we pulled up to them, and I wondered if Ryo had been keeping an eye out. Must have, or else I doubted they would have allowed twenty bikers with rumbling Harleys through.

I stopped near the front doors and climbed off. I heard the door opening a moment before Katon raced out. He shot down the steps like he was a twentysomething in a marathon, and I was the finish line.

"Sir... Sorry, Ruin, it's good to see you're back." Before I could say anything, he rushed on with "Master Ryo has instructed for me to take you to the meeting room."

"It's already started?" I made my way to the door with my brothers at my back.

Katon hurried after me. "They've only walked into the room."

"All right." I nodded.

I heard a few brothers comment on the place as we walked through the halls, but I didn't take in what was said.

Katon stopped at the door. "In here," he whispered just as a voice rose inside it.

"Thanks, stay out here," I told him. I opened the

door abruptly. It shot inward and banged into the wall behind it. I stepped through, the brothers following.

"What's the meaning of this?" Akio bellowed.

Taro stood at the end of the long-arse table in shock. If he didn't close his mouth soon, I would make good use of it. I caught Ryo smiling beside him and shot him a chin lift. It caused Taro to snap his mouth shut and glare at his friend.

As soon as I was close, though, his attention flashed back to me. "Josh."

"Hey," I said and leaned in to kiss his cheek. The brothers had fanned out around the room, standing behind Taro's family, who still sat in their chairs.

"What are you doing here?" Taro asked.

I smiled and took his hand in mine. "You'll see." I faced Akio and announced, "The Hawks MC wanted to let the Takahashi family know that with Wolf as head of the house, he has our support." Taro's hand tightened in mine. "In other words, anyone who wants to fuck with Wolf, fucks with us, and we don't mess around in reaping retribution if someone is foolish enough to screw with Wolf. The Hawks MC protects what's ours in any way necessary. No one wants us as enemies... the way we play is dirty. I'll be stickin' around to make sure that whoever is stupid enough to come after Wolf thinks otherwise."

"This meeting is adjourned," Taro announced.

Akio stood. He eyed the brothers and then looked to Taro. "You are not fit to run this house. Jiro was right."

"Why? Because I'm gay?"

He screwed his nose up. "That's one reason. You need to step down and let me be head of the Takahashi family before you destroy it with all your changes."

"I thought we were done with this when I dealt with Jiro," Taro said.

"It will never be done until you do not stand at the head of the table trying to control us in foolish ways."

"How is anything I've done foolish? Because I refuse to allow the men of the family to bargain off their daughters in marriages that they would never be happy in?"

"It should be the men's choice in what they want to do within their own family," Akio shouted.

"Careful with your tone," I warned.

"Or what?"

"Or I'll make you," I clipped.

The guy sitting beside Akio stood. "You dare speak to my father like that?" He pulled a gun and pointed it my way. His lips thinned, and his burning eyes shone with anger when I started chuckling.

"Wrong move, motherfucker," Vicious said from behind Akio's son as he pressed a gun to the back of his head.

"If you don't like the way I run things, then leave. Do not be foolish like Jiro was."

Akio stared Taro down, but Taro didn't move or flinch; he took it like the leader he was. Why were all the old fuckers wanting to live back in the dark ages? Times had changed, and if they had their way, it'd stay where the men looked down on the family's women. It disgusted me.

"We will speak of this at another time," Akio stated.

"No, we won't. You either walk from this room and leave or stay within the family and accept how I run things. The choice is yours, but you make it right now."

"Father—" The son started until Akio shut him up with a look. If he'd teamed up with Jiro, this dick could have possibly got lucky and taken over. But neither of them would have conspired to work together. Both of them were obviously stubborn and wanted to rule. Fucking idiots.

"We're leaving to go back to Japan," Akio finally said, and relief coursed through me.

"If that is what you wish," Taro said.

"I will not stay and be led by someone like you."

Taro shrugged. "I can't change how you think, Akio. I want you off my property by tonight."

Vicious moved back as Akio turned. He took in the brothers again before he stalked from the room with his son following and ten other men who must have been his people.

When the door closed, Taro called, "If there isn't anything pressing right now, I wish to continue this meeting another day."

The others stood, bowed to Taro, and walked from the room. The only ones left were Taro, Ryo, me, and the brothers.

"Ryo?"

"I shall warn your uncle in Japan of Akio's arrival.

Akio will be in for a surprise when he realises he's moved back to a place that has made just as many changes as you have."

Taro laughed lightly. "Tell Daishi Oji-san to record it."

Ryo grinned. His eyes shifted to me, and he nodded before he looked back to Taro. "Wolf," he said and bowed. He faced Talon and bowed again. I chuckled when Talon's eyes widened. He didn't know what to do or think about the cultural formality. Ryo walked from the room, closing the door behind him.

"Hey," I called softly, using his hand to tug Taro into me. "You all right?"

He sucked in a breath, keeping my gaze, and I caught the warmth in his eyes. "I am now."

"Don't ask me to go again, okay?"

He nodded, lips thinning, but I caught the slight tremor to the bottom one before he dropped his forehead to my shoulder. "Okay," he whispered.

"Don't worry, Wolf," Knife called. "You're not the only one with a fucked-up family."

Taro startled and straightened. A blush coated his cheeks. Had he forgotten they were even in the room? Taro faced Talon and bowed. "I appreciate the assistance."

Talon dipped his chin down before he crossed his arms over his chest. "You know why we're here, right?"

Taro looked back at me. "Josh."

"Yeah, Ruin. Know it's only new, but he's wantin' this

between you two, and since he's claimed you, we'll have his back, and yours. It's how Hawks works. We're all family. The partners are equals. There may be things we can't tell our partners, but we do it to protect them. Still, they're important in our lives, and I know you are for Ruin." Talon smirked. "Means we'll have to put up with each other."

"I am honoured to not only have the Hawks MC in my life but for trusting me with a member of your club. Thank you."

The brothers smirked. Some chuckled. Dad stepped forward. "Your words are cool, but just know if you fuck Ruin over, we're gonna be comin' after you with everythin' we've got."

"Jesus," I cursed with a groan. "Taro, I'd like you to meet my dad, Stoke."

It was comical how wide Taro's eyes shot open. A few brothers laughed.

Dad stepped forward and jutted his hand out, which Taro took and shook. "I promise to take care of your son. I care for him deeply."

If I wasn't around the brothers, I would have grabbed him and kissed the fuck out of him.

"You'd better," Dad said gruffly.

"All right, enough of that. How about we get some food goin' before you get on the road again?" I suggested.

Beast snorted. Knife laughed outright before he said, "Meanin' he wants us gone as soon as possible so he can get down and dirty with his man there."

Taro turned beet red as I slung my arm around his shoulders. "Shut the fuck up, Knife."

"Agreed," Dad said and then quickly added, "I don't give a fuck you two are dudes. It's just wrong hearin' about my son doin' the—"

"Dad, just no."

"Lunch," Taro blurted. "Katon," he called, and the door opened to a smiling Katon. "Lunch for all of us, please."

Katon bowed. "Of course, Taro-sama." He quickly disappeared.

As the brothers started talking, I pulled Taro aside. "Are you okay?"

He gripped my tee at my stomach. "Honestly?"

I nodded. "Yeah."

"I'm perfect because you're here."

I cupped the back of his neck and dropped my forehead to his. "We'll talk more soon, but know I ain't goin' anywhere."

"I wasn't thinking when I sent you away."

I pressed a finger to his lips and then tugged on his hair. "Talk soon. Let's get rid of my family first."

He pulled back and nodded, smiling softly. "You're lucky to have them."

Grinning, I glanced back to see them talking amongst themselves. Only Dad was watching me, smiling to himself. I sent him a chin lift, which he returned. "Yeah," I said, looking to Taro again. "I am lucky." But I wasn't only talking about my family. I meant it for the man in front of me, who opened my eyes when I didn't know they'd been closed.

"Come on. Let's get them fed." I curled my arm around his shoulders again and pressed my lips to his temple. He relaxed against me.

"Any other day I would be intimidated being in a room full of bikers."

Knife stepped up and punched Taro in the arm. I glared at him, which he ignored when he said, "We can still mess you up a bit if you want."

"I think I'll be fine. Thanks for the offer though."

"Anytime."

The door opened, and Ryo stepped through, holding it for Katon and a few other servers who held trays full of food. "Holy fuck," Knife commented. "I think I want to move in here."

"Not happenin', brother." Shit, I didn't even know if I was living here. Taro and I had a shitload to sort through, but I wasn't in a rush. For now, all I needed to know was that he was protected from his fucked-up uncle, and we'd be spending the night together.

Now *that* I looked forward to.

CHAPTER TWENTY

WOLF

I had never had many people in my life who made me feel like I was worth something. When I saw Josh stalking into the meeting with his club brothers, I knew he saw more in me than what I saw in myself.

I was enamoured by him.

I had worried he would see sense when he went home. But he hadn't. He was back, and just after one night. I couldn't stop looking at him as he sat next to me, talking and eating with his family. When he glanced my way with a gentle smile, my body reacted. My pulse raced, stomach tingled, and my cock throbbed.

His hand slid to my thigh and squeezed as he spoke

to his father. I couldn't look away. How had I become so lucky to have Josh here with me? Wanting to stay.

Ryo leaned into my other side. "You look like a lovesick puppy."

My face heated. "I do not."

Ryo laughed. "The men have stopped speaking to you because you didn't answer, only stared at the man beside you. He's real, Wolf. He's here for you. Let that sink in."

I couldn't because having him as mine seemed too farfetched. What did he see in me to come back? For Josh to have told his family about me meant so much. I couldn't believe he'd decided to do it, and all within a few hours being home.

Ryo was right. I did need to let the knowledge Josh was here for me sink in. The man had proved enough already that he wanted me in his life.

"Were the others really speaking to me?"

Ryo grinned. "Some."

"You should have nudged me."

"They didn't care."

They didn't either, else they wouldn't be sharing a meal with me. I never thought I could be this happy. But here I was, full of the warmth Josh provided for me in everything he did.

As with every relationship, we wouldn't always see eye to eye, but when we did fight, I would make sure we made up in the best of ways. Already I didn't want us to be apart again.

The past twenty-four hours had been a nightmare.

All my insecurities played with my head, but most of all, I had been scared I'd lost Josh by pushing him away. I knew he could handle difficult situations; the ones we'd already had showed me so. It didn't stop me from wanting to protect him though. But I figured in the end, we could have each other's backs. I wouldn't push him to leave again, and definitely not from the fear that'd coursed through my body and heart when I thought of him in danger.

Further down the table, Talon stood. "Let's hit the road." He turned to me. "Thanks for lunch. No doubt we'll see you again."

I could feel Josh looking at me. I squeezed his hand. "You will," I told Talon.

The Hawks men started filing out as I stood with Josh. His father was the last to leave. "Call your mother," he ordered Josh.

"I will."

Stoke glanced from his son to me. "Take care of him."

I tipped my head down. "You have my word."

"It's not forever," Josh said. "I still gotta come home and get my shit...." He looked to me, eyes wide a little. "That's if—"

I gripped his upper arm and told him, "You are moving in."

He smirked. "That an order?"

I grinned. "Yes."

"I'll need to find a job."

I nodded. "I'm sure you will."

"You've always got work within the Hawks," Stoke said. "You know that."

"Yeah, I know, Dad."

Stoke's jaw clenched. He reached out, and I let go of my hold on Josh for Stoke to tug him forward. They rested their foreheads together. "Love you, kid."

"Back at you, Dad."

With a slap to the upper arm, Stoke shifted away.

"Please thank Talon again for his assistance. I will forever be in debt to the Hawks MC."

"It's all good, Wolf. Just do good by him." He thumbed towards Josh.

"I will."

"He'll try to at least, but he gets on my nerves sometimes," Josh commented.

I glared at him. "You mean you get on *my* nerves."

Stoke grinned and told Josh again, "Call your mum. I'm gonna have to bring the tribe here, you know that?"

"Shit," Josh groaned.

I elbowed him. "They're more than welcome."

"Babe," Josh said quickly, covering my mouth with a hand. "You have no idea what you're sayin'. Mum will dote, Nary will question, and Rayne will think now I'm into a guy, that we can do nails and make-up."

Unable to resist, I pulled his hand away and started laughing. Wiping my eyes, I said, "Again, you are all more than welcome."

Along with Stoke's smile, he sent me a chin lift, and with another pat to Josh's arm, he made his way to the door where Ryo stood waiting.

"I have cancelled everything for the day," Ryo announced. "If something comes up, I'll deal with it," he added and bowed before he closed the door after Stoke and himself.

Josh faced me, smiling. He tipped his chin up. I noticed it was something the Hawks men did a lot in communication. The gesture was cute. Josh said, "Hey."

Shaking my head, I laughed. "Hi."

"Hope you didn't care about me interruptin' the meetin'. I wasn't gonna let another uncle of yours fuck with you."

"How did you know— Ryo," I bit out.

"He's just lookin' out for you, and I was already gonna head back here today anyway. I'd made the wrong move by leavin'. I know you were stressed and worried, but I should have fought, and I hate that I didn't." He stepped closer to place his hands on my waist. I let out a gasp when he lifted me and planted my arse on the table. He nudged his way between my legs. "This is new between us, but I wanna see where it can go, Taro."

I thumped my forehead against his chest. "I want to as well. So much."

"Good. Now, I need you to know I won't be leavin' again when shit gets hard." His hands slid to my back, one rubbing up to cup the back of my neck. "You sure you're cool with me stayin'?"

Lifting my head, I tilted it back to have his eyes. "I'm more than okay having you here with me. Like you said, this is new, but... I hated not having you in my bed last night. I hated I pushed you away. I won't do it again, Josh. I want you to be mine, for however long it'll last. Besides, you haven't even fucked me yet."

His eyes darkened before he dipped in to claim my mouth. I gripped him to me, locking my legs around his thighs, and deepened the kiss. My heart thumped hard in my chest. One day I would accept how lucky I was for Josh taking a chance on me, but until then, I would enjoy the ride we had together.

Josh threaded his fingers through my hair and tugged my head back, kissing down my neck. I shoved my hands up under his tee and vest, wanting, no, needing, to touch his warm skin.

He nipped at my chest, just above my shirt, and before I could do anything, he'd gripped it and ripped my shirt open, baring my body to him.

"Josh," I uttered as he kissed down to suck a nipple into his mouth. "Bedroom, now," I demanded.

He grunted against my flesh and licked around the other nipple before he took it between his teeth and bit down. I groaned, and with my hands, I forced his hips against me, feeling his erection caress mine.

I slapped his arse and growled, "Bedroom." I did not want anyone to see how Josh made me come undone or him lost in desire. That was for only me to see.

Josh grumbled but moved back and lifted me off the table easily. His muscles bunched and moved. I couldn't wait to see them shift when he took me for the first time.

Panting, I pulled my shirt closed, but as soon as I

dropped my hands, the sides parted. I glared up at him. "This was a favourite shirt."

His grin was cocky. "I'd say I'd buy you another, but it probably cost a few hundred." He kissed my nose, and I melted at the adorable move.

"I'm going to have to walk through the house like this."

"The fuck you will." Lifting his hands, he patted down my hair and brushed the strands from my face. He grabbed my shirt and pulled it closed. It opened right back up. "Shit." Josh glanced around. What for, I didn't have a clue, but he obviously didn't find anything when he scowled back down at my shirt.

"You should have stopped me," he snapped.

I snorted. "So this is my fault?"

His lips thinned. "Well, no." He scrubbed a hand through his hair. "You'll just have to walk behind me, holding your shirt closed so no one will see you."

"Are you serious?"

"Yes," he hissed. "Or do you want me to punch everyone who looks at you?"

I didn't think that would go down well with my employees. "No," I admitted.

"Good. Let's go." He took my hand in his, and I used my free one to hold my shirt closed. At the door, Josh opened it and peeked his head out. He glanced over his shoulder as he dropped his hand. "Stay close."

A laugh fell from my mouth. It was like we were on a mission. I winked, saying "Yes, pet."

He grinned, kissed me once, and moved out the

door. I stayed close behind him and nearly collided into his back when he stopped suddenly. It was then I heard voices.

Botan and a few other men rounded the end of the hallway. Josh crossed his arms over his chest, and I looked to see him glaring. Rolling my eyes, I pushed at his back.

Botan stopped. "Taro-sama, is everything all right?"

"It's fine," Josh answered.

Botan glared at him. "I wasn't speaking to you."

"Too bad," Josh retorted.

I pushed at his back again. Holding my shirt closed tighter since I had a feeling, from the hostility Josh was emanating, that he would punch someone if they caught sight of my chest. I thinned my lips, desperate to laugh since I had never had anyone act possessive of me before. Strange how it had made me happy.

"We're fine, Botan," I told him and gave another shove to Josh's back. He started forward again.

"I don't like that guy. He's always had a problem with me," Josh said.

Oh….

"Um, it could have something to do with you being in my bed. Botan was once a lover."

Josh halted immediately, only that time he turned and started off after Botan. Laughing, I grabbed his arm. "Stop." Smiling, I said, "He never meant anything, just someone to pass the time with, and it was a long time ago."

"Fucker," Josh snarled. "No wonder he was a dick to

me the whole time. He saw somethin' between us." He glared down the hall, and I glanced over to see the other men had moved on, but Botan stood scowling at Josh.

I ran my hand up Josh's chest. "Forget about it."

"He'd better not try anythin' with you, or I'll kick his arse." That I believed. Josh's hands slid to my arse cheeks and gripped. He pulled me close, our groins rubbed, and I sucked in a breath, wrapping my arms around his neck. I heard a noise down the hall but ignored it because Josh kissed me. It wasn't soft, but hard—a declaration to the other man that I was his.

I liked it. A little too much.

Josh pulled back, and I blinked dazedly. He smirked at me. "I think he got the message."

Grinning, I shook my head at him. I couldn't scold him for his actions. If it was the other way around, I would have done the same.

"You could pee on me," I offered. "Though, I do prefer this instead."

His brows dipped. "Wait, so I need to? How many guys have you slept with in your security?"

Fuck. "Ah...."

"Jesus Christ, this place will be a bloodbath. I want their names, where they work—"

I placed my hand over his mouth. "How about you remember that none of them meant anything. No one, until you. I don't care about them like I do you."

He glared and removed my hand as he sighed. "Fine. I suppose I can't kill them all off since they do help guard you and this place. Just get Ryo to make sure none of them look at you like they want a piece of you, or I won't be held responsible for my actions."

I smiled. "Have you always been this possessive?"

His head jerked back, and he was silent for a moment. "No," he said softly. "Never seen the point before. No one mattered that much to me. Until you."

My heart swelled in my chest.

I took his hand in mine and dragged him down the hall and all the way to our bedroom. Thankfully, we didn't run into anyone else.

CHAPTER TWENTY-ONE

RUIN

$\mathcal{M}$y words said to Taro had meant something. That was clear by the urgency in his steps as he dragged me towards and into the bedroom. All I could do was grin like a fool because I finally fucking understood what I'd been missing. The others in the Hawks MC had found, even Coyote, their someone who they'd do anything for, who they would protect at any cost, even if they had to use their own body. Their person who drove them wild and brought out their possessiveness.

Mine was definitely Taro.

I'd never acted this way with anyone before, and the knowledge of him being my one cemented itself inside me.

I kicked the door closed as soon as we'd entered and spun Taro around.

I needed him.

I grabbed his hair and tugged his head back to have his mouth in a hot and fiercely demanding kiss. Taro moaned and pushed his hands up under my tee, running them over my skin, making me shudder.

I would finally have him.

He would be mine, and I couldn't wait.

I just hoped I didn't embarrass myself by blowing a nut too quickly, because if my dick could talk, it'd be singing the song "Happy" by Pharrell Williams.

Wolf

Our kisses tapered off to pecks, until Josh caught my gaze, both our breaths heavy. "I'm gonna fuck you," he stated, his voice rough and dark.

My already hard cock throbbed. "Yes," I answered breathlessly.

Josh stepped back and removed his vest, gently laying it on the back of a couch. He kicked off his shoes and removed his socks. I quickly did the same and then watched him. He reached behind his neck and dragged his tee up and off his body, throwing it to the floor. I scraped my top teeth over my bottom lip, drinking in the sight of him.

"Shirt off," he ordered.

I slipped my arms from the already open shirt, and it slid to the floor. Our chests rose and fell rapidly at the anticipation of knowing what was to come. I followed Josh's hands as they went to his jeans. When he popped the button, I swallowed thickly. His gorgeous cock would be on display soon. Josh slid the zipper down, hooked his thumbs in the waistband, and pushed his jeans down. There were no boxers in sight.

I raised a brow, and Josh smirked. "I was in a hurry this mornin' since I knew I was comin' back to you."

My heart skipped a beat. I rushed to get my pants undone and down off my legs, along with my boxers. As I kicked them to the side, Josh chuckled. I took a step towards him, then paused. I... I had to get myself prepared for him. I didn't know if Josh would be turned off if I did it in front of him or not, since he was new to this with a man and not a woman. Though, I could be fretting over nothing. I didn't know, and I hated second-guessing myself.

His hands cupped my cheeks. I jolted a little but met his gaze. "Where did you go?"

My cheeks burnt. "Sorry, I just have to slip to the bathroom."

His brows shot down. "Why?"

"To, ah, you know, get ready."

"Huh?"

"I have to prepare myself for you."

It dawned on him, and his eyes widened a fraction. "Why do it in the bathroom?"

"I wasn't sure if it would be something you would want to see...." If it would be too gay for him or if he'd prefer for me to deal with it so he could just fuck me.

His reply was to tug my hips forward, causing our hard cocks to rub against each other. I sucked in a sharp breath when his hands gripped my arse cheeks. He went further and lifted me. I let out a yip but managed to wrap my legs around his waist and arms around his shoulders. No one had ever picked me up like this before. I found I liked being manhandled.

"What are you doing?" I asked breathlessly.

His smile was wicked. His eyes lit in a way I hadn't seen. One of his hands dipped lower. A finger slid in and caressed against my ring. I tightened my arms and legs around him as a shiver took over my body.

"Josh," I whispered, dropping my forehead to his shoulder.

"You ain't takin' away part of this experience from me," he told me gruffly. His finger disappeared, and I heard Josh spit before his finger reappeared wet as he ran it over my hole once again. I shuddered.

"All of this, all of you, is mine, and I'm all in. With everythin'. Got me?"

Smiling, I nipped his shoulder. "Got you."

He grunted, "Good." A finger gently and slowly pushed in. "Fuck, you're tight." His hands went to my waist, and I was lifted from his body. "Get on your knees on the bed," he ordered before he moved around me to my bedside table, which he opened and took out the lube. He glanced to the bed, saw I wasn't there, and turned to glare at me. "Bed, now."

My smile deepened even as my pulse raced. Josh placed his hands on his waist and watched me as I leisurely climbed on the bed, all while never taking my eyes off him. I ran them over his taut body, his hard cock that I couldn't wait to give attention to.

Josh kneeled on the bed beside me. I could have purred when he ran a hand over my back and arse. "Christ, you're hot," he muttered.

"So are you," I said softly.

He rested a hand on my shoulder and applied pressure. I sank to my chest, leaving my arse up in the air, which was how he wanted me if his hissed-out breath was any indication. His hand rubbed over my cheeks before he slapped down. I moaned from the sting.

Opening my eyes, I glanced back to see him slick two fingers up with lube. My cock throbbed. Already I was too close to the edge, because this was Josh. This was him taking care of me, getting me ready for him to fuck me.

All of it was a turn-on. Especially when I watched Josh as his hand disappeared and I felt his fingers glide over my entrance. He dragged his top teeth over his bottom lip, and his eyes darkened once again.

He didn't push them in though, just took his time rubbing, teasing. He shifted closer, grinding his dick into my hip. God, he was getting off on just touching me there.

"Josh, please," I begged, needing something of him inside me.

His gaze hit mine. He grinned when I shuddered. A moan tore out of me as he pushed a finger inside. "Yes," I hissed as pleasure hit my balls and gut. I near launched off the bed when he hit the right spot. "There, fuck, right there." I jutted back on his finger. "More, need more, pet."

"Fuckin' hell," Josh uttered, but he gave me what I wanted. Another finger joined the other. I hummed under my breath, but in the next second, when his fingers hit my prostate, I whimpered and pushed back on his hand. Fucking myself on his fingers.

Josh's lips hit my lower back, my arse cheek. He nipped and used his free hand to glide over my skin, up and down my back and shoulders.

"You," I demanded. "I need you." I was too close. I wanted to finish with him inside me.

"Yeah? You sure you're ready?" His tone was harder than normal, deeper.

"Yes, please," I panted.

I lost his fingers while his other hand gripped my hip, and he ground his cock into me. "Want me to take you from behind?"

"Any way you want."

"Fuck, I want you in all ways," he said, voice thick with desire as he shifted around me to rub himself into my arse.

Smiling, I got to my elbows and looked over my shoulder at him.

He cursed. "Don't look at me like that. I ain't gonna last as it is, but with that look, even less."

Chuckling low, I told him, "Take me then, pet. Need you to fill me up."

His upper lip lifted as he snarled, "Fuck." A condom appeared in his hand. Where he got it from, I didn't know or care. He looked down as he rolled it on. Next, I heard the lid to the lube pop open and knew he was covering his cock in the substance. His gaze lifted. "Ready?"

"More than ready. Fuck me, pet."

He groaned. "Okay, don't talk or look at me unless you want this to end now."

Laughing, I shook my head and looked down to the bed. Humour had never been on the cards when I was in the bedroom with someone, until him, and I fucking loved it.

Before he took me, his hand slid around my hip to the front, where he gripped my aching cock, waiting for the release I knew was coming.

"Goddamn, you're still hard."

I edged back, rubbing my arse on his cock, and told him, "Knowing it's you about to fuck me had me—"

"Shush," he ordered, drawing out another light snicker from me. That was until I felt the tip of him at my hole. He gripped my hips, slowly pushing in.

I dragged in a breath and relaxed my body, taking him in slowly.

"Fuck me, fuckin' hell. You're so damn tight."

I peered over my shoulder and found Josh staring

down at where he entered me. He swallowed. Sweat pooled on his chest and forehead. He was being patient for me, taking care of me, helping me adjust.

I wanted him inside me though. Now. I pushed back and groaned right along with Josh when he was fully embedded inside me.

"Taro, Christ, you okay?"

I hummed under my breath. Smiling over my shoulder, I blinked dazedly; the feeling of being full satisfied me a lot.

"Fuck me, pet," I uttered.

Josh cursed under his breath. His hand tightened even more on my hips as he pulled out, nearly to the point of losing him. I whimpered before he thrust back in.

"Yes," I cried.

"Jesus," Josh hissed. "You like that, don't you, baby?"

I nodded. "More."

"You want me to fuck you hard and fast, baby?"

"Please," I panted.

Josh pressed his lips to my back, where he said, "I'm gonna give you what you want." He moved. I lost him for a moment and looked to watch him get to his feet and crouch behind me. He gripped his dick and lined up, filling me once again. I moaned. Josh pressed his hand to my lower back and then proceeded to fuck me hard and fast.

I fisted the sheets and held on while Josh pistoned in and out of my arse like he owned it. Which he did. I would be more than willing to give myself over to him any time he wanted if he proved to me, like he was now, that he could own it.

I closed my eyes, trying to catch my breath, but it was hard to find with the way Josh drilled into me, and I loved every thrust he took. He kept hitting the perfect spot, driving me and my body crazy. My balls drew up, my gut tingling, and my legs shook.

"Taro, Christ, so good. You feel so goddamn good."

"Close, I-I'm close," I warned.

Josh grunted. "Same." His hand ran up my back, and he used all the strength he had in his legs and hips to keep fucking me. I wished I had a damn mirror above us so I could see all of him. I wanted to watch his body move.

"Josh," I cried just as I wrapped my hand around my shaft and stroked the cum out of me.

"Fuck. You're tighter." He cursed again right before his cock swelled inside me, and he came, gripping my hip and shoulder.

Panting, Josh slowed until he gently pulled out. Breathing hard, I collapsed to my side, only to find my arse full once again with Josh's fingers. I groaned and shuddered as he rubbed against my prostate.

"Pet," I whimpered.

He curled into my back and on his elbow so he could look down at me. His teeth grazed my shoulder as he moved his fingers in and out of me slowly. "Wanna come inside you without anythin' between us."

"Yes," I whispered, body tingling at the thought of having his cum in me.

"You're gonna get sick of me."

Confused, I dipped my brows and looked up at him, found him smirking. I asked, "Why?"

"I'll never get enough of this arse. It's my new favourite spot."

Smiling, I rolled my eyes and shook my head. My eyes crossed when he pushed his fingers in and hit the right spot again. "Josh," I groaned.

"Could you come again?" he asked.

I could, but he had fucked me well and proper. "Are you trying to kill me?"

He smirked. "With pleasure."

"I-I'm a little sensitive," I admitted, my body heating.

Josh pulled his fingers free and cupped me there before he shifted down to kiss my arse cheek. "Soon then, my pretty."

"Oh my fucking God," I cried incredulously. Did you just talk to my arse?"

"Forgot you were here," he teased. Scowling, I swatted at him. He laughed, wrapping me up in his arms so I lay half over him. With a kiss on my forehead, he said, "I did okay, yeah? I wasn't too rough, didn't hurt you?"

I melted on the inside because that was the most endearing sentiment I had ever heard.

My heart fluttered.

Kissing his chest, I laid my head back down and told him, "I loved every second of it, and no, you didn't hurt me. I wanted it hard and fast. You delivered."

"Good. I fuckin' loved every second."

Giddiness like I hadn't felt before spread through me. Grinning, I pressed my face into Josh's chest and squirmed against him.

A low chuckle dropped from him. "What?"

"You" was all I said.

His arm tightened around me for a moment. "Yeah, I get it, because it's you too who makes me happy."

Honestly, this guy would kill me with sweet words, and I would willingly go along for the ride.

CHAPTER TWENTY-TWO

WOLF

I stood in the kitchen with Ryo as we went over the day's details while having a much-needed coffee. Josh had kept me up the previous night after sweetly offering me a relaxing massage. Of course, it turned into more when he started massaging my behind.

It was a couple of weeks ago when he'd said my arse was his new favourite spot, and he'd proved it every chance he got. He couldn't keep his hands to himself.

Not that I minded.

"There he is," Josh called from behind me as he walked into the kitchen. I looked over my shoulder to see his eyes were on my arse.

"Ah...." Ryo muttered.

"I'm here, baby. Do not fret," Josh said, dropping to his knees behind me and cupping my arse cheeks.

Ryo's eyes widened. "Is... is he talking to your arse?"

I huffed out a breath. "Yes. He has a new fascination. Usually, it's behind closed doors though."

"I do not need to know," Ryo quickly said.

"Miss me?" Josh asked, and I felt his lips press against the top of a cheek.

Sighing, I said, "Josh."

"Hmm?"

"Stand up," I ordered. He was adorable and yet so very annoying. But also endearing.

Josh stood and curled an arm around my chest, dragging me back. "Mornin'," he said against my neck, where he took in a deep breath. His head lifted. "Oh, hey, Ryo."

"Maybe it's best you don't molest Taro-sama's arse when you don't know there are others in the room."

"He would have known," I replied, taking a sip of my coffee.

Josh shrugged and moved around me, heading for the coffee pot. "Yeah, I knew, but it's only you."

Ryo opened his mouth, closed it, then opened it again and said, "I don't know if I should be offended or not by that."

"Don't be," Josh answered. "Since I know you don't have a thing for Taro, to me you're like an ornament that's always around. Guess you could say I'm used to you, so I act normally in front of you."

I snorted.

Ryo narrowed his eyes. "Again, should I be offended? An ornament?"

I waved a hand around. "It's a compliment. He's comfortable around you. It's not everyone he would grope my arse in front of."

"Well," Josh drew out as he stared at me with heat in his eyes. "When your arse calls to me like it does, I won't care who's around. Speakin' of which. Ryo, do me a solid and make sure no one comes in here."

Ryo choked on his coffee before he swiftly started around the counter to exit the room.

"Ryo, come back," I said with a laugh.

"Don't do it, Ryo," Josh called. He put his mug down and moved towards me.

"No." I grinned, my hands coming up to fend him off. "Pet, I mean it. I'm still tender after last night."

Josh's smile was wicked. "You know what it does to me when you call me pet."

Rolling my eyes, I couldn't keep the smile from my lips so, of course, he wouldn't take me seriously. As soon as he was close, Josh reached out and dragged me into his arms.

Shaking my head, I rested my hands against his upper arms and told him, "You're hopeless."

He threaded his fingers through my hair and tugged my head back, lips moving to my neck. My hair was another part of me Josh couldn't get enough of. He loved the feel of it, and often when we lay in bed together, he played with the strands.

"I'm hopelessly obsessed with you."

My heart skipped a beat. I was the same with him. Everything about him drew me in, made me want him more as each day passed.

"Josh," I said softly.

He hummed against my skin, his hands sinking down to grab my arse and pull me into him. Both of us were already hard, and I sucked in a sharp breath as we ground against each other.

"I have a meeting to go to," I said before he captured my mouth with his in a searing, deep kiss. I wound my arms around his neck and thrust into him.

A knock sounded on the door.

"What?" Josh clipped.

"Wolf has a meeting in fifteen minutes," Ryo called through the closed door.

I smiled. "Told you."

Josh's eyes heated even more as he covered my cock with his hand. "Can't have you hard in the meetin' then." He dropped to his knees and started to undo my pants.

"Josh, we— Oh, fuck," I moaned, head dropping back when he sucked me into his mouth. His tongue swirled at the tip, a hand dragged from the base up to draw out the pre-cum. Looking down, I lifted my shirt out of the way and watched him fuck my dick with his mouth.

He excelled at it. Fucking. Whether mouth or cock, my man used both well.

A hand cupped my balls and gently rolled them, only to slide further between my legs and glide two fingers against my seam. That was all it took. Pleasure burst throughout my body. I gripped the back of his head and took over, thrusting into his mouth as I came.

Josh took it all. He even searched for some more by gently squeezing the last drop out of my tip and onto his tongue. Reaching out, I gripped the counter and breathed deeply. Josh stood and smirked as he did up my pants and straightened my shirt.

"You have about eight minutes now." The smartarse loved that he could have his way with me. I did as well, but I wasn't telling him that.

"What about you?"

"Huh? I don't have a meetin'. I've got to head to the compound, remember?"

Nodding, I curled my arms around his waist and kissed his neck. "Not what I meant, but be safe riding. If this new club isn't something you want to manage, you know I have a heap of jobs around here for you to do."

He tugged the ends of my hair. "I know, but... you know." He shrugged.

I did. Josh wanted independence, and I understood that. Already he had tried to talk me into helping pay for the utilities, but I refused. The main cost was from my family. He didn't want to work for me either, suggesting it would look bad with the family and employees I already had. As he put it, he didn't want any special favours because we were sleeping together.

"I do," I told him. "Good luck then. I hope it works out."

"I'll see what they say, where they're thinkin' of

buying the club. If it ain't close, I won't take it 'cause it means less time around you." His hands grabbed my arse. "And this beauty."

"Wolf," Ryo called, his tone a little panicked.

After a quick kiss, Josh lifted his chin towards the door. "Go, before you give him a heart attack."

Laughing, I started for the door and glanced back to see his eyes were glued to my arse. Rolling my eyes, I told him before I opened the door, "I'll take care of you later." I dropped my gaze to his still evident erection.

He winked. "Lookin' forward to it."

Once I'd opened the door, I stepped out, my cheeks warm when Ryo gave me raised brows. We started down the hall. "I do love that you're happy, Wolf, but it might be best to leave the bedroom activities to the bedroom. Then I won't have to guard a door and have to listen to the sounds you and Ruin make."

My face heated more. "It's not my fault." God, I sounded juvenile.

Ryo scoffed. "You didn't exactly stop him."

"It's hard to stop him."

"I do not need to know, but like I said, it's good to see you happy."

Smiling softly, I nodded. "I have never felt like this before."

"I know. I've seen you with men in the past, and none of them brought out this side of you." Ryo pulled the door to my office. "Now it's time for business. Do you think you can keep your mind on it?" He smirked.

I glared. "I'm not that bad."

"Says the man who stared out the window yesterday while his cousins tried to speak with him."

He had me there, but that was because Josh had been outside washing his bike, shirtless.

My phone rang on my desk. It was a call I had set up a couple of days ago. One that would change some of the businesses in the Takahashi family. Ryo slipped around the desk and answered it on speaker, "Wolf's office."

"Link here" was said gruffly.

"One moment, please." Ryo put him on hold and met my gaze. "Are you sure this is what you want?"

"Yes. It'll be better for the future. Not only for the family but for Ruin and me."

Ryo nodded and handed me the phone. "Link, Wolf, thank you for taking my call."

"Only taking your call because Talon mentioned your name. What do you need?" I had spoken to Talon a couple of days after they'd left and asked him if he knew of anyone he trusted in the illegal side of businesses. Someone who would be interested in some ideas I had. The next day, Talon had called back and given me Link's name and number.

"Actually, I have a business proposition for you."

"Know who you are. Heard of the Takahashi family. Consider me intrigued."

"I'm hoping you would be interested in taking off my hands 80 percent of my drug and gun trade."

"Eighty percent? What happens with that twenty percent?"

"I would become a silent partner. I want nothing to do with the businesses, but I figured since the Takahashi family worked hard to gain the clientele in the first place that we deserve something still."

Link snorted. "If you take 10 percent, then we can talk further."

I smiled, expecting as much; it was why I had started at twenty to begin with. I had been putting off this decision for a while, but it was crunch time. I wanted to try and get this family clean.

Talon had promised me Link would be trustworthy to deal with since he'd been business partners with Travis, Talon's brother-in-law, before he sold everything over to Link, who now ran the most successful prostitution ring in Australia. If I asked to be a silent partner, and we all agreed to the terms, it would work out without Link stabbing me in the back at some point. Talon would never have given me his name in the first place if there was a chance otherwise. And I trusted Talon, as he would do good by Josh. Talon also liked the idea of me getting the family out of the spotlight when it came to those businesses, for safety's sake. Again, because of Josh. I agreed with him, of course. Josh's safety, along with my family's, meant a lot to me.

It wasn't like the Takahashi family would suffer for money. We had other businesses, like transport, restaurants, and our anime stores, to bring money in, and they did.

"I'll agree to 10 percent."

Link whistled. "I'd like to meet the person you're doing this for."

I stilled. "Who says I'm doing it for someone?"

Link chuckled. "No one, but I can tell. If you've spoken with Talon, you'll know about Travis. He got out of it for a woman."

I hummed under my breath but said no more.

Link snorted. "Got it loud and clear. Whoever it is, is off-limits. Get some paperwork together, prove to me these businesses will be worth taking off your hands, and we'll do dinner."

"I'll get it done. Dinner will be set for Monday next week at the restaurant Tokyo. Seven p.m."

"Got it, see you then." He ended the call, and I placed mine back in its holder.

Turning to Ryo, I asked, "Did you hear that?"

"Yes. It's good you started at 20 percent."

"Especially when I only wanted ten."

Ryo nodded. "Are you positive he'll keep you out of it?"

"Talon and Travis are. Once he accepts, and I'm sure he will, we'll have to get word out the Takahashi family isn't linked to the gun and drugs trade."

"I'm sure the news will spread without us having to lift a finger. When are you going to tell Ruin?"

I smiled. "Once it's done. He'll be annoyed, believing he's responsible for this new direction, but I'll have him understand it was something I had been hoping for, for many years. I'm tired of how my father fucked this family over and how we've always lived on the edge, wondering when the next rival would come at us."

"It's a good move. Will Link be able to keep safe when the rivals realise we no longer hold the cards?"

I shifted my gaze from the computer screen up to Ryo. Was that interest in his eyes? "By any chance did you see Link's photo?" Ryo was bisexual, but I wasn't sure anyone else knew because he was a very private person.

His jaw clenched. "It's my business to know everything about a man you'll be dealing with for your safety."

I smirked.

Ryo scowled. "I may have seen his photo," he admitted. I couldn't blame him for being attracted to Link. If I didn't have Josh, I might have thought the same. Link was older than us, very good-looking, and covered in more tattoos than even Josh.

Although Josh had the perfect number. When I'd asked about them, he'd explained they all meant something. His body was a piece of art, one I loved to look at every chance I got.

"Do you know you get this soft look on your face whenever you think about him?"

"I do not," I clipped, knowing I was full of it. Even when Josh annoyed me, I still wanted him close. "One day you'll find someone, and when that day comes, I can't wait to hassle you about it."

"I will never be as... smitten as you are with Ruin."

"Just wait." I grinned. "Now, don't you have work to do, like myself?"

"Do you remember how?"

"Do you remember how I kick your arse when we spar?"

Ryo rolled his eyes and bowed. "Of course, Wolf. Call me if you forget something."

"Get lost, Ryo."

He walked towards the door. "Taro-sama," he called, hand on the doorknob.

I looked up from the computer. "Yes?"

"You do this family a great honour by leading it."

I smiled softly. "And you do this family a great honour for assisting me. I never did thank you for contacting Josh that day when I doubted myself."

Ryo tipped his chin down. "You're welcome."

Really, I would be lost without Ryo at my side. One day soon, I hoped to see him as happy as I was.

CHAPTER TWENTY-THREE

RUIN

I'd gotten a text from Taro earlier about having dinner together. As I walked into the house, my gut filled with those damn butterflies at the thought of seeing him. I made my way into the smaller dining room and found Taro sitting at the head of the table, reading over some papers. I stopped and took him in.

His eyes scanned the sheet quickly, and he nibbled on the corner of his mouth in thought. He wore the same shirt he'd been in that morning, so I knew black pants covered his legs. The thought of his pants reminded me of his cock in my mouth, and my cock thickened.

At some point that day, he'd tied his hair back in a

loose ponytail. Fuck, I loved his hair, more so when it flowed free around his face and shoulders.

"Are you going to stare at me all night, or can we eat sometime soon?" he asked without looking up from his work.

Grinning, I made my way over and stood beside him. I gripped the ponytail and tugged his head back. His smile was bright but quickly disappeared when I leaned in to claim his lips in a heated kiss. All while I removed the elastic from his hair and ran my fingers through his locks.

Pulling back, I asked, "Miss me?"

"Always," he breathed, eyes glazed over in desire.

"Good." After a peck to the lips, I sat next to him as he shifted the paperwork to the side.

"Katon," Taro called.

Like magic, the old man appeared in the doorway and bowed. "Taro-sama?"

"We'd like dinner now, please."

"Coming right up."

"Thanks, Katon," I added.

Katon smiled and went to bow at me, only to still. His smile grew as he walked off. Taro drew my attention back to him when his hand covered mine on the table.

"How did it go today?"

I grinned. "I'm gonna take it. The place they're buyin' is not far from here. It's gonna be a twenty-four-hour club. Figured I'll take the day shift since you'll be workin' as well. Someone else can do the night shift, but if they're in a bind, I'll help out."

"Sounds perfect. How many days a week? Or will it include weekend work?"

"Since I've got the experience in managing a place, they've given me the first choice on days. I've picked Monday to Friday. Since you were talkin' about taking the weekends off, I wanted to do the same."

His eyes softened. It meant something significant to him that he was behind my decisions. I wanted this to last between us, so would do all I could to make this work. There'd be struggles like in all relationships, but we'd pull through. Even if I had to strap him down to the bed and make him see reason or beg for forgiveness if I'd done something stupid to piss him off. It could happen. I did tend to annoy people.

"Are you happy you found something?" Taro asked.

"It's like a weight's been lifted off my shoulders."

His gaze shifted down to our hands clasped together. His lips thinned. "You don't miss Ballarat?"

I shrugged. "I might at some point, but I don't right now. If I do, we'll head there for the weekend or somethin'. I mean, that's if you can without a mountain of security comin' with us."

"Hopefully they won't." He nodded. "If you miss anyone, they're welcome here."

Lifting our hands, I kissed his knuckles. "I know, baby. I'd just worry that once Rayne sees this place, she won't want to leave."

He laughed lightly. "I'll be okay with that."

I snorted. "I won't. We'd never get any privacy."

When the food arrived, I gave his hand one last kiss before the plates were placed in front of us. My stomach growled from the aromas hitting my senses. Taro thanked his people, and they disappeared.

"I could marry your cook," I mumbled around a mouthful.

Taro glared. "Not that it will happen, but I'll let the cook know you enjoy her food."

Grinning, I devoured more food and then asked, "How was your day?"

"Same as always. Though, I heard from my uncle in Japan. He's already complaining about Akio since Akio doesn't like the changes Uncle has made."

"I remember you and Ryo sayin' something about this uncle. How's he changed things?"

Taro smiled. "My uncle is fifty and has only just come out of the closet. Discrimination in the family held him back."

Snorting, I shook my head. "Akio definitely won't like that."

"He doesn't. Which is why he's moving to the United States and starting his own faction. Not that he'll get any support from my uncle, nor me. I don't think Jiro or Akio understood how hard it is running a family and all the businesses that come with it. They enjoyed the money they received each month, but it was their children who helped out working."

"I doubt they know the work that goes into it. You mentioned your father didn't share information a lot."

He nodded. "There was a lot I never knew until he knew he was dying and had to pass on the information. I doubted he confided in Akio or Jiro since he never trusted them with the basic business things."

"Your dad's a fool for not havin' the help. Thank fuck you have Ryo, but you know if you need more help with shit, I'm here. I know I got a job, but that's only gettin' started on renovations. Even if it wasn't, I'd still make time to help you."

Taro's hand slid across the table and rested on my arm, where he squeezed. "You do understand that if we stay together—"

"There ain't any *if* involved."

His eyes lit. "Sorry, my mistake. You do realise that since we're together, everything I have is yours also. The house, the people in it, even the workers. There will be times I'll reach out to you if the pressure is getting too much, but for now, I have things handled."

Wait…. "Are you sayin' I run this place as much as you do?"

"Yes."

The thought of being equal in this place and businesses kind of freaked me out, but it was sweet Taro wanted that between us. Like we were already married and not starting out. I'd see down the track how it went, if I could adjust to the knowledge of being seen by his people as an equal beside Taro. For now, all I could think about was… "Meanin' I could fire someone?"

His brows dipped, and he said hesitantly, "Yes."

"Then I'll inform Botan it's his last night here."

Taro chuckled, shaking his head. "Josh."

"Do I need a list of who else there was?"

"We've been over this. There has been no one as important as you are. Before you, it was all a fog, and it only lifted when you came into my life."

Christ.

That got me in the chest. I'd been thinking of a question the last couple of days, and hearing him say the words made me want to know the answer even more. His response could bring us closer again.

"Fine. I'll concede."

He smirked. "Thank you."

"Can I ask you somethin'?"

He nodded, picking up his glass. "Anything."

"Do you like to fuck or are you just a bottom?"

His sip dribbled from his lips as his eyes widened. He quickly wiped at his chin as Katon and his crew appeared to clear the plates.

"Taro-sama, is there anything else we can get you?"

Taro shook his head but said nothing.

"We're good, thanks, Katon," I told him, keeping Taro's gaze. Colour built on his cheeks, and I wondered what he was thinking.

As soon as the others had left, Taro swallowed. I watched his throat work as he licked his lips.

"Well?" I asked.

"Both ways," he whispered.

"So, if we went to the bedroom, you'd fuck me?"

His eyes flared. "If that is what you want."

I chuckled; he was unsure if I really wanted his cock inside me, but I did. I'd been thinking about it for a while. I loved arse play, so I guessed I'd enjoy feeling him move inside me.

"Yeah, baby, it's what I want."

Taro stood abruptly. His chair tipped backwards and crashed to the floor. "Bedroom, pet," he clipped. Before I was even out of my seat, Taro started walking from the room. Laughing, I stood and followed him. He kept glancing over his shoulder to make sure I was still behind him. Taro left the bedroom door open for me, and I stepped through. Only he wasn't in sight. That was when I heard the shower running.

Grinning like a fool, I went into the bathroom and found him naked, standing under the spray of the steaming water with a bottle of lube in his hand.

My brows rose. "In here?" I took off my clothes quickly, eager for this to happen. My cock sprang free and hit my stomach, already hard.

"We'll start in here, but we'll finish in bed."

I pulled the door open and joined Taro in the shower. His hand wound around my wrist, and he dragged me into his arms, lips meeting, fighting for dominance.

Panting, Taro pulled back and told me, "The mail came today."

"Yeah?" I didn't know where he was going with his statement, too busy enjoying his hands running over my back and arse.

"Yes." He bit my earlobe before sucking it into his

mouth. I shuddered. Taro ran his tongue around the outer edge of my ear. "Know what I found?"

"What?"

Taro shifted to my side. "Hands on the wall, Josh," he ordered. I did, spreading my legs wide. My gut tightened, and my cock throbbed as I watched him squirt some lube onto his fingers. One hand wrapped around my dick and jerked up and down. The other he used to rub a couple of fingers over my hole. A shiver raked over my body.

"I forgot to mention what I found in the mail."

Slowly, he dipped a finger in. My arse fought the intrusion for a moment, until his hand on my cock distracted me. His finger slipped all the way in, and I cursed when it hit me right where I wanted it.

Taro kissed my shoulder, my neck, and after teasing me, he worked another finger inside.

"God, Josh... I can't wait to be inside you." His voice was low, rough.

"Then fuck me," I demanded. I wanted it, him, his cock... everything. Already the pleasure was intense, and I needed him inside me before I came.

"Not yet," Taro said, kissing my shoulder again. I tipped my head to the side and caught his mouth, fucking my tongue inside. Taro moaned, his fingers working my arse, but the other had stopped jerking me, and I was grateful as fuck, sure I would have lost my load ages ago.

I pushed my arse back onto his fingers, wanting him

deeper. "Taro," I growled when it didn't feel enough. "I want you."

His fingers slid out, and Taro shut off the water, ordering, "Dry quickly."

My arse damn hummed from the attention, but my cock ached for its release. I wiped the water away as I watched Taro do the same, his dick standing to attention.

"Josh, you keep distracting me, and I forgot to tell you something."

"What?" I asked, following him back into the bedroom. Another bottle of lube sat on the bedside table, but there were no condoms. "Wait, you're kidding me? We got our results?"

Taro spun my way, smiling. "Yes."

My body goddamn tingled at the thought of having Taro's bare cock inside me, feeling his cum.

"Christ, yes." I fist-pumped the air and launched onto the bed. "Let's get this show on the road."

Laughing, Taro shook his head, his eyes shining with warmth and desire. Lying on my back, I put my hands behind my head and asked, "How do you want me?"

He grazed his bottom lip with his top teeth. "Like that. Spread for me, pet."

The action was strange, but I pushed my legs out, and his eyes zeroed in on me. Reaching down, I stroked my cock and watched him slowly move onto the bed on his knees.

"You really want me to fuck you?"

"Yeah, Taro. Want to try it all."

"If you don't like anything, let me know, and we'll stop. You can fuck me."

"Oh, we'll be doin' that later 'cause I want my cum drippin' outta you, but I want you inside me, baby, and I know I'll like it 'cause it's you."

His body rolled as he crawled towards me. "The things you say, pet." He dipped to kiss one thigh, then the other. Taro proceeded to kiss, nip, and lick all the way up my body. Our eyes met. We smiled softly at one another, my heart skipping a beat.

He was *mine.*

All mine.

Thank fuck I'd taken a chance on this. On him.

Taro reached for the lube and kissed me again before sitting back on his haunches. I shivered when his hands gripped my inner thighs and spread my legs wider. Breathing deeply, I watched him cover his fingers in the liquid before moving it between my legs and hissed when the coolness dripped between my cheeks. I shifted to my elbows to see Taro gently rubbing it around while he used the other hand to lather up his cock in lube.

My neck arched when he slipped a finger back inside me and pumped it in and out. I lifted my arse and rocked with his movements. Another finger joined the first, and I dropped my head back and moaned when he teased me in the right spot.

My dick was about crying for release, but I wasn't ready—I didn't have Taro in me. "Taro," I bit out.

His smile was teasing. "Yes, pet?"

"Get your dick inside me. Now."

"Anything you wish," he said, voice husky. His palm pressed into the bed beside my head. "Lift a little." I did and felt him at my entrance. He pushed in a little, and I goddamn gasped. It was different than the fingers. Bigger. Harder. Taro kissed my temple, my cheek. "Breathe, pet, breathe."

Sucking in a breath, I nodded.

"Look at me," Taro ordered. Lifting my gaze, I saw the strain on his face and knew all he wanted to do was thrust in me to get clamped on. I'd felt the same way the first time inside him, but Taro wouldn't want to hurt me. There was something to be said about a little pain; it was a rush to the head. Chasing my need, I gripped his arms and pushed down on his dick. He slipped in further. Another rush hit me.

"Taro," I groaned.

His eyes flared as if understanding what I was feeling. "More?"

"All of it," I ordered.

Taro bent, kissed me, and thrust inside. I groaned around the kiss and held him tightly to me, grinding up onto his dick.

Panting, Taro pressed his forehead to my shoulder. "Oh fuck, pet, you feel so good."

I hummed under my breath and rubbed his back when he pulled slowly out and plunged back in.

"Fuck me," I cried when he hit my prostate and ground against it.

"I am, pet. I am." He pulled out again and pushed back in. I gripped his hair and tugged his mouth down to mine. That was when he lost control and fucked me into the bed like he'd been possessed. His hand wound around my right thigh. He brought it high and went deeper.

"Christ," I grunted against his mouth before tangling our tongues together in a hot and wet kiss. "Baby. Baby, close," I warned. My body tensed, my arse tightened around him, and I was coming in the next second without even touching my cock.

Taro groaned, pulled back, and got to his hands above me. I kept coming with every thrust. Taro made a noise in the back of his throat, and he swelled inside me, drawing a strangled cry from me, and I felt his seed coating me inside.

Gently, he pulled out but stayed between my legs. I opened my eyes, breathing heavily and feeling the loss of him. His gaze was between my legs. His hand dipped in. I shuddered when he slipped a finger inside, pushing his cum back in.

He bent, kissed my stomach. "Never had better," he mumbled, pulling his finger free. I wrapped my arms around him, tugged him down, and rolled so I half lay over him, resting my cheek to his shoulder.

"This was where I was always supposed to end up," I told him, honestly believing it.

"Josh," he whispered, curling his arms tightly around me.

"Don't get tired on me, baby. As soon as I'm ready,

I'm gonna fuck you, 'cause I wanna see *my* cum drip outta your arse."

He chuckled, rubbing my back. "Then lift your head and kiss me so we can get started."

I did.

CHAPTER TWENTY-FOUR

RUIN

*B*y the time I left the club after overseeing some renovations, it was late. There was no need to rush home, though, since Taro would be out at a business dinner. I walked down the street towards the car park area not far from the club and passed a Japanese restaurant. The scent drew me in. I was starved. Knowing there'd be plenty of food at home didn't stop me from looking in and drooling over the plates I saw on people's tables.

I stopped. "What the fuck?" I snarled. My eyes caught on Taro sitting at a bar with some tattooed guy.

They talked.

They smiled.

Even laughed.

Anger slipped into my veins.

Shaking my head, I took a deep breath. I had to remember Taro said he was out to dinner on business. This guy was business. What type of business? Because I sure didn't like the way he was looking at Taro.

Like he wanted all of Taro's business.

I could be exaggerating, but I knew a player when I saw one. Hell, I used to be one, and we recognised our own kind. He had it written all over his face.

What type of game was this dick playing at, though?

The guy chuckled at something Taro said and put his hand on Taro's arm. I saw red, clenching my teeth and fists. I locked my body down to stop from waltzing in there and pissing on Taro while growling, "Mine."

A waiter blocked my view. "Move, fucker," I clipped as I near pressed my nose up to the glass. I could feel people staring at me, but I didn't give two hoots.

When the waiter walked off towards a hallway, Taro and the piece of shit got off their stools and followed him.

Why were they going out the back?

Were there private rooms out there?

Grabbing my phone, I googled the restaurant and rang the line. A female voice answered, "Tokyo, how can I help you?"

"Question, if I was to book a meeting, are there any private rooms available to eat in?"

"Of course, sir, there's—"

My anger built as I ended the call and scowled through the window. Why did they need a private room? I didn't like it. There wasn't anything I liked about what I saw. Where the hell was Ryo? He was supposed to have his back, even when guys were flirting with Taro. He had to stop that shit. I'd have to talk to him about it.

So now what was I supposed to do? Did I go home like a good little boy and wait for Taro to return and explain what the fuck was up with this? Or did I wait for him outside so I could keep an eye on the fucker to make sure he didn't follow Taro home? Another option was to walk in there to make sure the piece of shit knew Taro was taken and to quit the flirting.

I trusted Taro.

Completely.

I knew all he wanted was me. I was a damn catch, after all. Yeah, I was also cocky enough to see it written all over him. He was smitten like a kitten, and I felt the same way about him.

The problem was other people.

I didn't trust other people I knew nothing about at all.

The guy looked rough. Looked like he could overpower Taro and fuck him on a table.

I strode to the door and opened it.

WOLF

. . .

IT WAS easy to get along with Link. He was laid-back, funny, and smart. I was glad Talon had suggested him.

"Here we go, gentlemen," the waiter said, opening the door to a private room. He dipped his head at me, knowing I owned the restaurant. Link walked in and looked around. It was a small room but good enough for the four of us. Ryo and Link's guard showed up after I entered. They'd been standing back from us at the bar, checking the area.

Link took a seat at the table; I followed suit. Ryo stood behind me. Even when I offered him a seat, he suitably shook his head. Link hadn't offered his guard a seat, though. The guard whispered something to Link, who nodded, and the guard left the room.

"He's going to make a call." He leaned forward, elbows to the table, hands clasped. "Want to get down to business before we eat?"

"That would be good. Did you get a chance to go over the paperwork I emailed this morning?"

He nodded. "I did."

I waited, leaning back in my seat. We'd already ordered our food at the bar while waiting for the room to be cleared.

Link smirked, his gaze briefly shifting over me to Ryo and back again. On the inside, I was cheering that he looked at my friend. I wanted him to notice Ryo. Upon seeing Link in person, Ryo had reacted in a way I'd never seen from him before... by tripping.

Keep looking at my friend. He needs your attention. Fuck the business. He's worthy of your time.

I couldn't say or do anything, unsure what type of look he gave—if he had been checking Ryo out or sizing him up. The man was difficult to read.

"I'd like to accept the deal, but I want to confirm all rights for the businesses will be in my hands."

"Everything, yes."

Link nodded. "It's a fuckin' large amount of money. Are you sure you want to give it up for some person?"

"You obviously haven't met the right person to be willing to do such a thing for. Though, it's also for my family. You do understand the attention this will bring upon you? Our family has always dealt with rivals wanting to take our business."

Link grinned. "You don't need to worry about that. Most are too scared to deal with me. My reputation speaks for itself." I had heard he killed without any remorse, and he was also intimidating to others because the number of men he had on his payroll was vast.

Hmm, maybe Ryo should look elsewhere for someone. I wouldn't want Ryo to be caught in any trouble being associated with Link. Then again, Ryo would call me stupid for underestimating him.

Voices rose outside the door. Ryo gripped my hand, pulled me from my seat, and planted me in front of the table while he then reached over and yanked Link out of his seat, pulling him to stand beside me. Ryo took up position in front of us, gun raised, pointed at the door.

Link's eyes glowed with humour. "Did he just manhandle me to protect me?"

I grinned, my own gun in hand, ready to see what was going on outside the door. "He did."

"Huh," Link grunted and stared at the back of Ryo.

"Sir, you can't go in there" we all heard.

"Like fuck" was snarled by a voice I recognised. "Move."

Ryo relaxed, as did I, and both of us put our weapons away. Link looked from one to another and back again before he asked, "What's going on?"

Ryo snorted. "You'll see." He moved to the door and opened it just as Josh pushed the waiter to the side and stepped through. "It's all right," Ryo told the waiter.

"You," Josh snarled, pointing at Link. "I don't give a fuck if this is some business meetin' I'm fuckin' up. You do not touch him." His finger shot to me. "He's mine."

My heart danced around in my chest, as did my stomach. Any other time I would be pissed, but since Link was Link, I didn't care.

Link turned to me. "You're fuckin' a Hawks member?" He laughed. "Shit, this is epic. No wonder he stormed in here, ready to kill me. Those fuckers are possessive."

The fight deflated out of Josh, and confusion dipped his brows. "You know Hawks?"

Sighing, I went to Josh and curled an arm around his waist. "Josh, this is Link. He's Travis's old business partner."

Josh huffed. "No shit."

Link held out his hand. "No shit. Whose son are you?"

Josh shook his hand and replied, "Stoke's."

Link nodded. "Met him at Travis and Vi's wedding. Think highly of the Hawks."

Josh grinned. "Good to hear." He rubbed at the back of his neck. "Ah, sorry about before."

"Nah, man, I get it. Not sure how you thought I was coming onto your man, though."

Heat hit Josh's cheeks. "Saw you two at the bar. My mind started overreacting."

Link snorted. "Heard it happens a lot with you guys when it comes to your better halves."

Josh chuckled. "Guess you could say that." Josh glanced at me. "Not sure what business matter you guys are talkin' about, but can you excuse us for a moment?"

Link chuckled and waved a hand. "Go for it." It was like Link understood what Josh was talking about, but I didn't. Not even when he dragged me out of the room and across the hall to the men's room.

He pulled me through the door and locked it. "What's wrong?" I asked him.

"Hands to the counter, Taro," Josh clipped.

"W-What?" I laughed.

"Hands to the counter, now."

"Josh—"

He crowded me, cupping my chin. His eyes held fire within them. "I didn't like what I saw. Know it's nothin' now, but it's still in my head. You two laughin', talkin', and when he *touched* you...."

My eyes widened. "Touched me?"

"Yes," he hissed. "A caress to the arm. It might not be anythin', but I need to fuck you to get it outta my head."

My pulse kicked up, my cock hardening from his tone and words of claiming. "Josh," I said softly. "It was nothing. I didn't even notice."

He pushed into me until my butt hit the counter and stepped into my space so our noses touched. "Hands to the counter, Taro."

Was I really going to let him fuck me in a restaurant bathroom?

Yes.

I kissed his neck and turned in his arms. I undid my pants and pushed them down with my boxers. I heard Josh's belt and zipper before I looked into the mirror and saw him gazing back.

"Lube?" I asked.

He lifted a tiny packet of lube in his hand before he bit the edge and tore it open. Josh applied pressure to my shoulder, and I jutted my arse out to him.

His fingers rubbed against my hole. I shook my head and said, "No foreplay. Fuck me, pet. Make me yours."

A growl rumbled out of him. He lined his cock up and gently pushed inside of me. My mouth dropped open in a silent cry as he filled me up.

Our gaze clashed in the mirror as Josh reached around and cupped my jaw. "Who do you belong to?" He pulled out.

"You." I whimpered as he thrust back in.

"That's right. Mine. All fuckin' mine." His hand wrapped around my neck, his mouth to my shoulder, and I held on as he fucked me hard and fast. Even when he kept his mouth on me, his eyes rose to meet mine. His other hand bruised my hip, but I didn't care. I loved every second of this carnal fucking.

Pleasure thrummed inside me. My balls drew up, and I wrapped my hand around my cock, jerking.

"Josh," I uttered.

His tongue licked at my ear. "Yeah, baby. Come for me."

That was all I needed to shoot my load over the front of the counter. Josh's mouth latched onto my neck and sucked. He swelled, groaned, and filled my arse with his warm seed.

When his hands loosened, his forehead hit my back as he watched himself slowly pull out, causing a shiver to rake over my body. Josh pressed in, aligning his front to my back, and his arms wrapped around my chest. We stared at each other. My lips twitched, and he grinned like the cat that ate the canary. He ground his softening dick into my arse.

"Are you good now?" I asked, raising a brow.

Josh chuckled and kissed my neck. "Yeah, baby. Very good." I moved to the stall to clean up, and a look came over Josh.

I shook my head, knowing what he wanted. "I can't leave your cum inside me. It'll leak out onto my pants."

His jaw clenched. "Yeah, I know."

I did what I had to and heard Josh washing up. When I stepped out of the stall, I walked over to him and hugged him tightly. "How about later you can come all over my skin? Mark me."

His eyes heated, and he brushed my hair off my shoulder. "Like I did here?"

I glanced to the mirror and found a hickey. I melted into his arms as a thrill ran through me. "Yes, mark me up more, pet."

He tugged my hair. Knowing what he wanted, I gave him my mouth. Breaking the kiss a few beats later, Josh asked, "Should I apologise for how I acted?"

I shook my head. "No, I don't think Link cares."

He pressed his forehead against mine. "You drive me crazy, Taro."

"Same, pet."

He straightened. "What's the business with Link?"

I smirked. "I was going to tell you later. But since you're here... which, by the way, why are you here?"

"The club's down the road. Was walkin' to my car when I saw you."

I nodded. "Not far from home at all."

He grinned. "No, it ain't. Now tell me what's goin' on."

"Link's taking over the gun and drug trade. The Takahashi family will become silent partners, only taking 10 percent."

His brows dipped. "Why? This ain't because of me or anythin'?"

"No... well, in a way, yes." He went to say something, but I covered his mouth with my hand. His grip on my waist tightened as he glared. I smiled. "I've wanted to do this for a long time. I never liked how Dad brought this trade into the family. It caused nothing but trouble. This will keep you safe, but also me and my family. It's best for everyone. Talon assured me Link would be the best to work with, so I reached out, and he's keen to sign the agreement."

He pulled my hand away after kissing it. "Talon knows?"

"Yes, I went to him for advice."

Josh snorted. "Of course he'd help if it meant gettin' the shit away from us. But are you sure, completely sure, this is what you want? What about the money it makes for the family?"

"Even without the guns and drugs, our family are billionaires with our other *legal* companies."

Josh's eyes widened. "Billionaires?"

I laughed. "Yes, pet, you're dating a rich man."

"You know I don't care about any of that."

I ran my hands up his chest. "I do. It's what drew me more to you."

A knock sounded on the door, and Ryo's voice called, "Your dinner is getting cold, Wolf."

"Coming," I said. "Are you okay now?"

"Fuck yes, but I'm stayin' for dinner."

Warmth spread through me. "All right." Together, we walked back into the room. Josh, of course, placed his hand on my arse on the way. Link thought it was hilarious, especially when he pointed out the hickey while Ryo rolled his eyes, but his lips twitched.

As we sat, Josh suddenly asked Link, "You gay?"

"Nah, mate. Just bi."

Josh grunted. "Know you know this guy's mine." He thumbed my way while I slapped a hand to my forehead. "But Ryo's up for grabs."

The room quieted. I glanced to Ryo and found him blushing and glaring at the ground.

"That so?" Link said.

"Yep."

"Thanks for the information."

Josh gave him a chin lift, and I pulled him in close when Link went to speak to the waiter who'd just entered. "How did you know Ryo was into men?"

"Caught them eye fuckin' each other when we came back in. Thought I'd help Ryo out. Then we'd get more time together."

Shaking my head, I laughed and kissed his shoulder. Yes, Josh definitely made me happy, and I wanted him for the rest of my life. I would make it happen; I just didn't know when.

All I knew was I completely loved him.

He was it. My future.

EPILOGUE

RUIN

*T*aro stood at my side at the front door while we waited for my family to arrive. They'd texted not long ago saying they were near. Only Taro couldn't seem to stay still. He shifted from one foot to another.

"What's goin' on?" I asked, taking his hand in mine.

He looked at me, biting his bottom lip. "We've been together for four months."

Confusion swamped me. "And?"

He grabbed the front of my tee and tugged me into him. "And I love you…. There, I said it, and I'm not taking it back." He shook a little. "You make me happy, you idiot, and I want you here forever." His chest rose and fell rapidly while my body reacted to his words. My heart swelled, my cock thickened, and my gut tingled in that special way only Taro could bring out.

Cupping his cheeks, I grinned at him. "Fuckin' love you too, Taro Takahashi, and I was gonna stay here forever whether you liked it or not. My life has only gotten better with you in it."

To my surprise, his eyes glistened, which touched my heart where it skipped a beat. He sucked in a shuddering breath and nodded. "All right then."

Grinning, I told him, "Maybe next time you tell me you love me, you can do it when we aren't about to have visitors so I can fuck you."

A smile grew on his lips. "All right," he whispered.

I watched as I traced my thumb over his bottom lip. "Still, I love that you told me."

"Okay," he said softly.

"Now kiss me to seal that confession in." His grin widened as he wrapped his arms around my shoulders and planted one on me. I gripped his arse and brought him in as close as we could be without melting into each other. Though at times I wished I could.

When we heard a car rolling down the drive, we broke apart, but I snuck back in for a final kiss just as we heard, "Holy shit, this place is the bomb."

"Rayne," Mum snapped.

"Rayne," Dad clipped, only lighter than normal.

Pulling the door all the way open, I took Taro's hand, and we stepped out on the front landing. I squeezed Taro's hand. "Just remember you invited them here." Though the invite had been through me since he hadn't met Mum as yet because he couldn't make it home when I went there a few months ago.

Taro chuckled. "I will."

Another car rolled down the drive. One I recognised. "You invited Nary and Vicious?" I called down to Mum, who blushed.

"Well, you see, your sister wanted to see where her brother was living and meet his man for the first time."

Rayne skipped up the steps and wrapped her arms around my waist. I dropped Taro's hand to curl mine around her shoulder. "Hey, sis."

"Hey, fool." She grinned up at me, then moved her gaze to Taro while Dad and Mum got their luggage out and waited for Nary.

"This is Taro. Taro, meet my pain sister, Rayne."

Rayne tipped her chin up. "Hey."

"Hi, Rayne, it's good to meet you."

"Are you sure you're into my brother? 'Cause I can take you off his hands and live here myself."

Taro sputtered out a laugh while I shoved my sister. "Traitor."

She shrugged, giggling. "What? This place rocks. I'm gonna spend all my school holidays here."

I shot Taro a look. "See what you've done inviting them?"

He tried to contain his laughter, but it slipped out anyway. "I do."

"Hello," Mum said, stopping in front of us. "I'm Malinda, Josh's mother."

"I'm Nary, his sister. Saxon said you've met him.

Same as Dad. But this is Ayra." Nary rubbed at her daughter's back as she held her on her hip.

Taro smiled warmly. "I have met the men. But it's good to meet the rest of Josh's family."

Mum elbowed me in the ribs. "You picked well. He's very good-looking."

"He can hear you, so don't go giving him a big head."

"Thank you," Taro said when Mum glanced at him. "Mimi said she's running behind but will be here soon." Ryo was also running late since he stayed over at Link's the previous night. Those two were fucking like rabbits, but every time I pestered Ryo about how things were, he told me it wasn't anything serious. I called bullshit.

"Great." Nary smiled. "No doubt Mimi will bring Cowboy. Those two are attached at the hip lately."

"She is," Taro said. He was happy his sister had found someone who doted on her.

"Can we get inside? I could use a drink from drivin' here and listenin' to Rayne's playlist," Dad said as he shook Taro's hand. Vicious stepped up and took Taro's hand in greeting as well.

Rayne rolled her eyes. "You've just got no taste, Dad."

Dad snorted. "Married your mum, didn't I?" Rayne shut her mouth quickly.

"Of course, my house is yours." We made it through the front door to where Katon stood. Katon bowed, and the women giggled, not used to being served or someone who'd bow to them. "This is Katon. If you need anything, please let him know."

"It's a pleasure," Katon said, straightening. "If you leave your bags, I'll take them to your rooms, and after some refreshments, I'll come to collect you to show you around."

"You rock, old dude," Rayne said. Katon blushed and smiled at her.

"We'll grab a drink in the library," Taro said. He nodded to Katon and patted his shoulder before leading the group to the library.

I stepped up to Dad. "How's Talon?" I hadn't seen him since I went home in a rush that last time after I found out our prez had been shot and was hanging on to his life in hospital. The fucker who shot him died, of course, but it'd scared everyone to the core. Hawks wouldn't be the same without Talon in it.

"He's good. Back at work like nothin' happened."

"Thank fuck." Even though I'd felt relief when the doctors told everyone he'd pull through, it was as if more lifted off my chest hearing how well he was doing. It could also have a lot to do with how close I'd grown up with the family, with Coyote being his son.

Dad's hand landed on my shoulder. "How's things?"

I smiled at the ground. "Good." Taro's words bounced around in my head. *I love you. You make me happy, you idiot, and I want you here forever.* "Real good."

"Glad to see it, son."

"How many rooms does this house have?" Rayne asked when we reached the library.

"Forty," Taro supplied. "But it's only because most of my family and staff live on these grounds."

"That's cool. Though, if I had a bae, I'm not sure I'd want my family around interrupting things."

"Rayne, there'll never be anythin' to interrupt at your house because you're never havin' a boyfriend, and you're stayin' home forever," Dad announced.

Mum glared at him.

Dad quickly amended. "Well, not forever, just until you're thirty. Then you're goin' to live with your sister."

Nary snorted. "Don't bring me into anything."

"We are not havin' another woman in the house. Two are enough," Vicious said.

Nary turned to him slowly. "What do you mean by that?"

Vicious saw his mistake. "Nothin', angel. You two are perfect, but your sister cheats when we play on the Switch."

"I do not!" Rayne yelled.

"Rayne, inside voice," Mum scolded.

I walked up behind Taro and wrapped my arms around his chest, tugging him back into me. "Regret it yet?" I asked into his ear.

His hands gripped my arms, and he turned his head. I met his lips in a quick kiss. Taro smiled bright and said, "Not at all. This is perfect."

It was, and I couldn't wait to see what our future held. For the moment, all I knew was that no matter where our time together went, I'd have Taro at my side. I seriously hadn't been lying before.

The guy was never getting rid of me.

ALSO BY LILA ROSE

Hawks MC: Ballarat Charter

Holding Out (Free)

Outplayed (standalone related to the Hawks MC)

Climbing Out

Finding Out (novella)

Black Out

No Way Out

Coming Out (m/m novella)

Out to Find Freedom (standalone related to the Hawks MC)

Hawks MC: Caroline Springs Charter

The Secret's Out

Hiding Out

Down and Out

Living Without

Walkout (novella)

Hear Me Out (m/m)

Break Out (novella)

Fallout

Hawks MC: next generation

Coyote

Ruin (m/m)

Texas

Standalones related to the Hawks MC

Out of the Blue

Out Gamed (novella)

Romantic Comedies

Making Changes

Making Sense

Fumbled Love

Bumbled Love

Polished P & P series (m/m romance)

Wreck Me Forever

Never a Saint

Working Out West

<u>Titles under L. Rose</u>

The Hidden Kingdom Trilogy

(reverse harem romance)

A Torn Paige

A Lost Paige

A Final Paige

Standalone's

Infinite Bond

www.ingramcontent.com/pod-product-compliance
Lightning Source LLC
Chambersburg PA
CBHW070547120726
47909CB00007B/2268